Wicked All The Way

With bonus story

Wicked to Love

Wicked Lovers Novellas

Shayla Black

Wicked All The Way
A Wicked Lovers Novella

Shayla Black

Published by Shayla Black
Copyright 2012 Shelley Bradley LLC

Edited by: Chloe Vale and Shayla Black

ISBN: 978-1-936596-18-8

Dedication:

As with any book, so many people help me along the way, but there are a special few I'd like to thank.

First, to Pearl for your excellent reading skills and the occasionally giggle that let me know I was doing things (mostly) right. To Laurie and Angel for your enthusiasm. You ladies kept me going during some tough days. To Chloe Vale for her excellent editorial guidance, as always. And not killing me for being last minute…again. Last, to my husband, who proposed to me during the holiday season many years ago. While the proposal may not have gone exactly as planned, the rest of our lives have been everything we could have asked for. Thanks for the inspiration for this story.

Chapter 1
Black Friday 2012 – Tyler, Texas

"If I have to watch you ogle my mother-in-law's ass for another second, I'm going to gack."

Caleb Edgington tore his stare from Carlotta Buckley's gorgeous backside wrapped in a soft black skirt and turned to glare at his oldest son, Hunter. He crossed his arms over his chest. "Like I've never had to watch you ogle Kata? You forget, you two visited me not long after you married. Want to know how much sleep I got those few days for listening to you newlyweds through the walls?"

Not at all repentant, Hunter just grinned.

Rolling his eyes, Caleb stole another glance at the object of his lust as she and her daughter, Hunter's wife, made their way around the garland-wrapped corner of the restaurant, heading up the hall to the ladies' room.

Damn, Carlotta's ass made him salivate.

He sighed. "You think you got the market cornered on attraction because you're married? Or young?"

"Nope. I'm going to gack because you've been staring at her ass for over two years, and you still haven't managed more than…what, two dates?"

A flare of heat passed through Caleb's system, partly fueled by anger that Hunter was throwing this shit in his face. The other part was a pure jolt of erotic sizzle. Yeah, two dates in two years. And the kiss that had ended that second one…

Caleb picked up his cell phone and bounced it lightly against the checkered tablecloth, gathering his words. "She's afraid of me."

Instantly, Hunter's teasing smile disappeared. "I thought you two had worked that out."

"As long as we're just 'friends.'" Caleb's lip curled up in annoyance. "Saying I wanted a hell of a lot more was a tactical error on my part that put us back at square one."

"Having met her ex-douche bag, Gordon, I can't say I'm surprised that she's reluctant."

"I'm not a damn thing like him!" And if Hunter thought so, Caleb wasn't too old to exert some parental ass-kicking influence.

"Oh, hell no. Not even close." Hunter scowled. "What I mean

is…you're on the forceful side. Where do you think Logan and I got that trait from, Dad? Granted, you taught us how to respect a woman. Gordon, that damn asswipe, treated her like she didn't matter. He told her what to do, when to do it, how to do it. After her driver's license lapsed, he refused to take her to have it renewed. With her ankle injury—which he didn't allow her to rehab—she couldn't take herself. He convinced her to quit her job. He cut her off from her friends, her livelihood, and the outside world. Remember, he didn't even fucking take her to the doctor when she had pneumonia. Instead, he tried to convince her that she had seasonal allergies. If I had to guess, I think she's just worried about letting another take-charge man near her."

"I might be a bit overprotective, but I'm not that kind of asshole," Caleb insisted.

"You're not, but smothering?" Hunter's stare challenged him to own up to the accusation.

Caleb just gritted his teeth.

"Remember when Kata and I went through something like this? My wife was only afraid that she *could* lose her identity, because apparently I can be a little overbearing. Who knew?" Hunter gave a mock shrug.

"The whole universe?" Caleb suggested with a grin.

"Yeah, just remember, you and I are cut from the same cloth."

No denying that. Hunter was a dead ringer for him twenty years ago.

"But here's the difference," his son reminded him. "Carlotta *did* lose her identity. Her fear isn't a maybe/might thing. It's real and in the not-too-distant past."

Caleb balled his hand into a fist. Hunter's words explained why she'd run and stopped nearly all contact between them, family dinners and minor emergencies excepting, after he'd pinned her against the door of her cozy little house and kissed her after their second date. He'd tried so damn hard to coax her gently, but Carlotta didn't just flip his switch—more like the whole circuit breaker of his central nervous system. With his lips layered over hers, he'd grabbed her screen door to restrain himself from hauling her into his arms and dragging her to bed. Caleb still remembered the horror on her face when she realized that he'd inadvertently ripped the little metal contraption off one of its hinges. She'd quickly slid in the house with a murmured good night and slammed the door in his face. After that, he'd done everything he could think of to reassure her—fixing her door, flowers, phone calls.

No response.

Had he given up? Not really. He'd plotted a tactical retreat…but every time he got around her, he was as subtle as an Assault Amphibious Vehicle. Of course, twenty-four years in the U.S. Army didn't exactly cultivate a talent for tact.

"I know," Caleb admitted. "When she stayed with me just after her separation, she nearly jumped out of her skin every time I even came near her."

"I think she's filed you in the 'overwhelming' category."

Exactly. But it didn't do him any good to pretend to be someone else in order to win her over. From everything he understood, her ex had pulled that routine.

"She's not leaving me with many options, but I'm not giving up. I've dated the alternative." Caleb grimaced. "The last one was forty, just divorced, and ready to skip dinner to tango between the sheets."

"Don't say another word, Dad. That is a textbook case of TMI." Hunter looked a little green.

Caleb wasn't a lot more comfortable saying it, but facts were facts. He'd gotten to the age where he appreciated a woman for qualities other than her sex drive. Not that he didn't want that, too. Being over fifty hadn't been a death sentence on his libido—at all. But Carlotta was just…more.

The waitress, wearing black slacks and a Santa hat, dropped off the check. He picked it up, waving away Hunter's money, as thoughts of the beautiful woman assaulted him without mercy.

Her tender heart drew him. Over the past two years, he'd noticed that she went out of her way to please just about everyone. She'd helped Kata decorate her first apartment with Hunter, turning it into a cozy little nest for newlyweds. Complete strangers at the hospital where she worked felt her compassion daily when she shared a smile, a tear, their silence. She'd taken to mothering Hunter with an affection he hadn't had since Caleb's own wife had walked out on him nearly fifteen years ago. His macho Navy SEAL son might not admit that he liked it, but when Carlotta cooked his favorite meals, Hunter preened like a cat basking in sunlight. She'd even opened her heart to his younger son, gently teasing or scolding

7

Logan whenever he was home and on leave. And the sweet woman had all but adopted Logan's little wife, Tara, and his youngest daughter, Kimber, both of whom had grown up mostly without a mother.

Carlotta spared him only stuttering words and averted gazes…and lots of blushing. Yeah, he made her nervous.

"Good. I don't want to talk to you about my sex life, either. But how am I supposed to convince her that, despite my hard head, I'd be good to her?"

Hunter hesitated, then whipped out his phone, sending a quick text. "Let me think on that, maybe talk to Kata. In the meantime, I've texted my gorgeous wife and told her to stall coming back to the table. I was hoping to ask you for a favor." On cue, Hunter's phone beeped. He read it. "All right. That buys me five minutes."

Caleb wasn't particularly ready to change the subject, but Hunter had suddenly turned antsy. Whatever it was, his son found it damn important. "Shoot."

"Remember when I came home at the end of May, then rushed back here in August?"

"Vaguely." Caleb shrugged.

"Kata was ten weeks pregnant and lost the baby."

The air left Caleb's lungs, and he leaned forward, gaping at his son. Then he scowled.

Hunter held up his hands. "Before you say it, I know. But Kata wanted to tell me first, in person, and I didn't get leave. I knew nothing until she called from the hospital. She didn't want anyone but her mother to know. That's just Kata. You know she doesn't want the pity."

"Oh, shit. I'm sorry, son." He clapped Hunter's shoulder gently, wishing that he'd have known or could have helped. Kata had an independent streak that his son had learned to respect—so he had to do the same.

"I won't lie; it's been a tough three months. I had mixed reactions to it all, but it's made me confront some things I've been putting off." Hunter sighed heavily. "I can't be an active-duty SEAL forever."

"It's a tough gig after thirty, I'm sure."

"Amen. Kata wants to have kids now. I'd planned to wait until I left the Navy. I didn't want…"

Hunter looked like he was grasping for diplomatic phrasing, and Caleb saved him the trouble. "What your mother and I had?"

"Yeah. She tried to raise three kids while you were gone. She was alone, angry, depressed. I know other women manage, but I don't want to risk putting Kata through what I fear might make her unhappy. And when Mom walked out because she couldn't deal anymore, I resented the hell out of her."

His son had summed up some of the problems, but he and Amanda had suffered through many others. He had been overbearing. Protecting her had been his way of showing affection. Well, that and taking her to bed. Amanda had wanted someone more charming, less rough around the edges. He hadn't known what to do with her tears and rants that life hadn't turned out as expected, so he'd shut down.

Caleb rubbed the top of his military-short hair. It was probably more gray than golden these days. Wasn't that shit supposed to bring wisdom? For the life of him, he didn't know what to say to his son.

"So I take it you've come to some conclusion?" he asked Hunter instead.

His son looked pensive. "Jack and Deke have offered me a job. Good money, health insurance, far less risk of dying in a third-world shithole."

"But you love what you do."

"Yep, but everyone knows I'm one injury away from being off the teams for good. This shoulder of mine has been shot up twice." He rolled it. "It's stiff. I worry… What if it freezes up on me during a mission? What if me wanting to hang onto this part of my life endangers a teammate? I worry about it, but…" Hunter fingered his phone, probably to avoid eye contact more than anything.

Like father, like son. Communication was essential, but they were both far better at sorting through others' issues. They tended to bury their own.

"Not enough to quit?"

"Nope. I just work out harder. Then I remember the six months I thought that Kata and I were divorced." Hunter drew in a shaking breath. "It fucking gutted me, and I couldn't go through that again. She wants kids. She wants a husband who's home more than not. She wants normalcy."

"And you think it's time you grew up and shouldered your

responsibilities?"

Hunter's blue stare bounced up to his. "Yeah. And actually, I'm finding myself looking forward to it."

"You're so much fucking smarter than me. I didn't figure out all that crap until I was over forty."

His son snorted. "Of course I'm smarter. That was a given."

Marriage had been good for Hunter. He was still intense as hell, and Caleb knew he was largely the cause of that. But he'd found his sense of humor, could talk about his feelings now, and worshipped the ground Kata walked on. In some ways, Caleb found himself a little envious.

"I'd be lying if I didn't say I'm ready for some more grandkids. Two strapping boys, and what do I have from them? Jack squat. Your baby sister has outclassed you in the reproduction department."

"That's where the favor comes in." Hunter drew in a deep breath. "I scraped together some of my savings, along with part of the last signing bonus I received. I bought us a house. I want to surprise Kata for Christmas."

"That's great, son. You don't think she'll string up by your balls for buying a house without her input?"

Hunter laughed. "Yeah, my wife does threaten that a lot. I'll just start reminding her that if she wants kids, then string and my balls don't belong in the same sentence...or the same room. Luckily, she's seen this house, likes the neighborhood. But the place needs work. It's older and been vacant. The kitchen especially shows it. I set aside another chunk of cash for some remodeling...but I have to be back on base in forty-eight."

And he'd have no time to tackle the renovation in the last few weeks before Christmas.

"You want to shamelessly use my handiness around the house?" Caleb teased.

"Absolutely. I've already changed the locks myself since there'd been squatters in it. I bought new carpet for the bedrooms. I've ordered some hardwood for the foyer, kitchen, and great room, and tile for the bathrooms. It should be ready for pickup tomorrow. There's another ten grand in the account tied to this debit card. I'll text you the PIN. Whatever you can do with this money and just over four weeks... I'd appreciate it enormously."

"You're a lucky SOB that I've embraced retirement and don't

mind home improvement projects." Caleb smiled.

Truth was, it would be nice to fill his idle thoughts with something besides getting Carlotta under him and spreading her pretty, round thighs so he could see her pussy. Touch it. Taste it. He had little doubt that she'd been celibate since before her divorce, and he'd play on the need wrought by her deprivation if he had to. But he'd rather start with holding her, building trust, making her comfortable and happy. Then he'd make her scream out his name.

"Whatever you're thinking, please don't share." Hunter gave a mock shiver, then tossed him the keys.

Caleb caught them with one hand and batted his son's head with the other. "Shithead. I'll help you with one condition."

"Shoot."

"Don't talk to Kata about her mother. I think…I've got an idea."

#

"Can I talk to you for a minute, Carlotta?"

At the sound of Caleb Edgington's voice behind her—how did he get that close without her hearing his approach?—she shivered. Butterflies in her stomach was something she hadn't felt since adolescence, and she didn't like how feminine he made her feel. His voice was always deep and rife with desire. He didn't hide his feelings well. Of course, she didn't think he really tried.

Though it had been over two years since her bout with pneumonia, she had never forgotten her recovery. Hunter and Kata, then newlyweds, had taken her from her neglectful ex-husband's home and brought her to Caleb to convalesce. He had carried her everywhere, simply scooping her up in his arms to cart her upstairs for sleep, then bringing her downstairs for meals. She wasn't a tiny woman, so how did that man manage to pick her up as if she weighed almost nothing?

Caleb cleared his throat, bringing her back to the present. She glanced over her shoulder. Though he hadn't spoken again, he all but compelled her with those terribly blue eyes, with the rugged planes of his face. Carlotta dragged in a shaking breath. The truth was, she owed him for all his gruff care while she'd recovered. Yes, she'd baked for him and given him a lovely card…but she'd purposely left everything on his porch when he wasn't home.

Because he made her blood race for the first time in forever. And he terrified her.

Gathering her oxygen and courage, she turned and looked up, up, up in order to meet Caleb's gaze. Even in the darkened parking lot illuminated only by the scattered lamppost here and there, Caleb still looked like something out of a fantasy. Those watchful eyes gave her nowhere to hide. His tight T-shirt attested to his daily multi-mile run. Bulging arms showed that he wasn't idle, as if he sought to prove that age really was just a number. He looked every bit as good as guys half his age.

He deserved someone a little less fifty, a little less round…a little less wary of relationships.

"Of course, Caleb." She pasted on a brightly fake smile. "I always have time for family. What would you like to talk about?"

The man blanked his irritation with a carefully impassive expression, but she knew that he didn't like being lumped in as a relative. And truthfully, she didn't see him as one—at all—despite months of trying. Yes, he looked like Hunter. Her son-in-law treated Kata very well and made her daughter one happy woman. Caleb…he just looked like a hugely capable, sexual man.

She swallowed against a little dizzying wave of desire as she stared at him and pretended disinterest.

Pretending became nearly impossible when he wrapped his hand around her elbow and brought her just a bit closer. Across the parking lot, she saw Kata and Hunter drive away. And there went her security blanket.

"Let's step into this little coffee shop."

He did not ask or wait for an answer, just started leading her in that direction. Carlotta weighed giving in to his demand against protesting. In the end, it wasn't worth the fight. They were going to be in public…and she liked his hands on her more than she should.

A moment later, Caleb led her up the curb, somehow mysteriously placing himself right where he could help her in case her ankle decided to freeze up, as it occasionally did. Then they were inside, surrounded by people of all ages with their laptops, mellow music, low lighting, and the smell of exotic coffee rife in the air.

He led her to a table in the corner, near the back, then seated her like a gentleman, pushing her chair close.

"Coffee? Dessert?"

"No, thank you. I am pleasantly stuffed after that lovely meal. Thank you for dinner."

"My pleasure. I'm getting coffee for myself. Do you want a smoothie? Water?"

So, he wanted her to have something to make her comfortable during a potentially long discussion. Carlotta sighed. What exactly did he want to talk about? Hopefully not to revisit their last date and that kiss that still made her feel hot all over whenever she thought of it. And made her fantasize about him touching her.

"Water, then. Please." She settled into the chair, studying the black, faux-wood table.

Caleb made his way to the counter, and she stared under her lashes at the sturdy width of his shoulders, the tapering of his lean waist to his narrow hips. He stood ramrod straight, like a military man, and kept his gaze trained forward while ordering from the twenty-something barista. He returned a few minutes later with his hands full. Once he settled into the chair across from her, she realized how small the table seemed, how quiet the corner was, how little air she had to breathe when he sat so near.

Goodness, if he asked her out again, would she have the fortitude to say no? Of course, she really, really wanted to say yes—to nearly anything he might ask. But if she couldn't handle a putz like Gordon, Caleb Edgington would run over her entirely. Keeping her guard up was critical.

After setting his steaming coffee aside, he palmed a big bottle of water. He'd thoughtfully asked for a cup, then poured some of the cool liquid for her. "Here you go. I'll get to the point. The kids need our help."

That disarmed her immediately. "Of course. Is everything all right? Kata said nothing to me about trouble."

"Not trouble." Caleb paused. "Hunter just told me about the miscarriage."

Surprise and irritation flashed through her. Her son-in-law knew well that Kata wished to keep this secret. She understood that he had likely found that difficult, but... Hadn't he and Kata not grown past Hunter unapologetically taking control of their lives?

Carlotta frowned and opened her mouth to protest, but Caleb held up a hand. It would have been a bossy gesture if his expression hadn't been so contrite. "I know Kata didn't want anyone else to know, and their secret is safe with me. Logan and Tara would be hurt, but…the kids have made a choice and I respect that. The information goes no farther."

"*Mija* can sometimes be very close-mouthed with things personal."

He leveled a glance at her that said "pot meet kettle," but didn't voice it. "Understood. Because of that incident and some discussions they've had about having kids, Hunter told me he's cooked up a surprise for Kata for Christmas. He's bought her a house in Lafayette."

Irritation dropped away, and a smile broke out across Carlotta's face. Her eyes teared up. Carlotta had loved Hunter from almost the first moment Kata had introduced them. Her son-in-law had rescued her from a terrible marriage. The young man just kept proving over and over how much he loved her daughter. A house represented a commitment to family and future.

"She will be thrilled."

"I'm glad you think so. This is where we come in. According to Hunter, the house needs work. I'm going to drive out there tomorrow and take a look at it, make a list of what needs to be done. I can fix just about anything, install new plumbing or electrical or whatever. I can even paint." He pressed his lips together, as if reluctant to admit there was something he couldn't do. "But I can't decorate."

Carlotta suppressed a grin. Kata was particular about that sort of thing. Caleb had done right to come to her for help. She alone knew her daughter well enough to pull together a style that would please both Kata's need for flourish and a touch of feminine, but still preserving the function and masculinity for Hunter.

"Thank you for asking me to help. Of course I will." She frowned. "We have very little time. Christmas is just a few weeks away."

"Exactly. While I'm there tomorrow, I'll text you a few pictures. Maybe you can start sketching some ideas. I'm going to look at the flooring Hunter picked out."

Carlotta tried not to, but she winced. Caleb laughed.

"Sorry. But in my experience, most men who try to decorate should not."

He grinned at her. "Myself included. I admit it."

Which surprised her, but nicely so.

14

With so little time before the holidays, they couldn't spare even an hour. Pulling together a single room could take weeks, let alone a whole house. "Actually, I am not scheduled to work for the next three days. If you would not mind the company, I could come out there with you and list out my ideas and what must be done."

It would be a nice respite from her own too-quiet condo. And if it made her daughter happy...then she could overcome her own discomfort at being in the company of a man who made her remember that she was still a woman.

Caleb smiled, and it transformed his stern face into something warm and mesmerizing. Carlotta found herself leaning closer, smiling back. A flush crawled up her cheeks, and she looked away, unbearably aware of his gaze on her. He was a smart man, so he must know that he affected her. Of course he did—but that knowledge did not make his pull any less potent.

"It's a long drive. Do you mind if we get an early start?" he murmured.

His tone felt almost like an intimate caress. How else could words that innocuous have the same impact as him saying, "Take off your clothes for me."

She blushed harder and tried to brush her reaction aside. Maybe wine with dinner had been a bad idea and was impairing her judgment.

"Early is fine. Did you have a time in mind?"

"Seven?" He sipped his coffee and sat back in his chair, giving her a bit of space.

The extra air should have been welcome. Oddly, she worried that he was no longer interested in her, and that she'd imagined his voice turning its seductive power on her.

Carlotta risked a glance up at him. No, she hadn't imagined anything. He might have given her more space, but his gaze drilled her with a blistering heat that made her catch her breath.

She swallowed back excitement. "Seven would be great."

Chapter 2

They rolled up to Hunter and Kata's new house early in the afternoon. The cab of his truck smelled like her. Something spicy and musky, but mysterious. And so damn feminine. It wasn't perfume or lotion or anything manufactured that he'd smelled on a million other women. He'd noticed it before…but cooped up in a small space with her when the weather was too damn cold to roll down the windows just magnified the scent. How the hell was he going to stand up now that they'd arrived without embarrassing himself or scaring her? Caleb rubbed at his eyes. He didn't think that telling her he'd been sporting the same erection since well before hitting the Louisiana state line would put her at ease.

"It is so charming!"

Carlotta's smile and glowing eyes didn't make him any less hard. Dragging in a deep breath, he forced himself to compartmentalize and focus on the house. On the corner in an established neighborhood with mature trees, it had a cottage feel. White with shutters in a pumpkin color. A wide porch held up by four slender columns shielded a host of flowering plants and a hanging bench swing. Big windows along the front, a white door with a leaded glass inset, and decorative silvery house numbers along the front all added to the cozy feel. It wasn't big, but Caleb could see why Hunter would want to call it home and maybe raise a baby or two.

"I'm sure they'll be happy here. Let's go see how much work the interior needs. The exterior looks good."

"The grass needs cutting." She pulled out a little notebook from her purse, along with a pen, and started making notes. "The little detached garage out back probably needs a coat of paint."

Caleb cocked his head to look down the line of the house. She was right. "I'll take care of that."

"They are lucky to have you." She smiled. "Helping, I mean."

Yeah, because Carlotta could have him any way she wanted if she'd just say the word.

That wasn't happening anytime soon. Sighing, he stepped out of the truck and jogged around the front. Carlotta had opened her door and was trying to hop to the ground in not-quite-practical heels and another one of those skirts that hugged her ass and drove him insane.

What he really wanted to do was put his arms around her waist and lift her against him. But she shot him another one of those skittish stares, so he merely offered her a hand. She took it, and her soft heat was a jolt through his system. Jesus, as if he could get much harder. The moment her feet steadied on the ground, Caleb forced himself to turn away and headed for the house.

Heading up the little walkway, he fished out the keys Hunter had given him and pushed open the front door. That's where the charm ended. He passed through a little foyer. Dark and cramped, with a strange little half wall that supported spindles up to the ceiling, it cut the opening off from the rest of the house. Maybe if there'd been a coat closet or something functional, he could see the purpose. But at six foot three, all he felt was cramped.

The parquet floors had seen better decades. Someone had broken into the house at some point and spray painted an interesting collection of obscenities low on the half wall.

"Oh, dear." Carlotta's voice shook.

That was one way of putting it. "I vote we rip out this pointless wall. It's not load bearing."

"It makes the house feel smaller."

"Right." Caleb wandered further inside. "The fireplace needs a good scrub."

She nodded. "Everything needs new paint."

True enough. The work of the graffiti artists continued. Their vocabulary belonged in the gutter. Carlotta winced.

"I'll definitely take care of that, too. I'm guessing…kitchen off to the left?" He put a hand to the small of her back and led her away from the insults in red-spray paint.

But the kitchen wasn't any better. Several of the cabinets hung crooked, dangling by a single nail. Some of the doors had been torn off, the shelves ripped out. The sink was filthy. The refrigerator had been rolled to the middle of the floor. Caleb was almost afraid to open it. He filed that project in the *later* category, then opened a mystery door, expecting a pantry. Instead, he peeked down, flipped on the switch just inside.

"What is it?"

"Attic."

Caleb took a couple of steps up and surveyed the room. "Partially. Someone left a bunch of junk here, but it wouldn't take much to toss it out and finish the room off."

It wasn't a huge space, but he could think of a use or two that would make Hunter and Kata happy.

Stomping back down, he turned off the light, then guided Carlotta into the dining room. Other than thrashed carpet and another multi-colored paint job, there was nothing wrong with the room. Down a little hall, and he ran into one bedroom with a cracked window, another one with a large closet that needed a little drywall repair, and the master bathroom, which had some water damage around the shower. This was more than a weekend project...but he liked the challenge.

Caleb glanced over to find Carlotta hesitant, then furiously writing on her notepad. "You okay?"

She blinked at him as if coming out of her own world. "Fine, yes. All is well. Ideas flying in my head. This bedroom and bathroom should be spa colors. The bedroom just across the hall would make a lovely nursery. Kata has a love of white kitchens. White cabinets with a white, solid surface countertop. Something with streaks of gray or earth tones. Once we have that in place, I'll have a better idea what color to paint the walls and what backsplash to choose. Something glass would be nice because she likes sparkle, but we will see what is available. What flooring did Hunter choose for the room? Did he leave us a budget?"

"Hardwoods. Yes, I've got it. How about we discuss more over lunch? I'm starving. You can tell me your ideas."

"You go ahead. I have too much to write out to leave now. I will be fine here." Subject dismissed in her mind, Carlotta turned with pen in hand and headed out the bedroom door.

Caleb frowned and gripped her elbow. His hand was gentle, but she wasn't getting away. "Did you eat breakfast?"

"I usually skip it."

He knew his frown became a glower, but he found her skipping meals unacceptable. "Not with me, you don't. And you won't be skipping lunch, either."

"I am a grown woman. I do not need you to tell me when to eat."

Wincing, Caleb let go of her arm. Since divorcing the ex-douche bag, Carlotta had guarded her independence zealously. Ordering her trampled on that. But he couldn't let her simply have her way.

"We have hours of very hard work ahead of us. You need to fuel your body or you'll be exhausted in an hour or two."

Her eyes sharpened, large brown pools that seemed to have no end. He could fall in there if it meant staring at her gorgeous face for the next hundred years. Time had been kind to her. The small lines around her eyes were faint. Her lips were still a plump, red bow. The curves of her breasts and hips were voluptuous. In the past two years, she'd grown her hair out so that it brushed over her shoulder caps in fat curls he wanted to bury his hands in as he guided her to his lips, his cock…

"I often eat but one meal a day. With hips such as these, I can afford to skip meals."

She spoke the words wryly and meant them as a joke, but they just pissed Caleb off.

"Not when you're with me." He brought her closer. "I still remember that fragile woman Hunter took from Gordon's house. He brought you to me and put you in my care. It's my duty to watch over and protect you. My son and your daughter would not be happy with me if I allowed you to run yourself down. I'll let you pick out whatever food you'd like, but we're eating now."

Carlotta dug in her very sexy heels. "I do not appreciate your bossiness."

"It's not the first time, and I doubt it will be the last."

Caleb ushered her out the door. She stomped and huffed, and in truth, he had to work not to laugh…and be a little proud. When Hunter had first brought her to his house, she'd been meek and willing to accept anything in order not to create waves. And to look at her asserting herself now? It made his cock hard. Then again, everything about her did.

Herding her out to the truck, he helped her up, then hopped into the driver's side. "Where's a good place to eat? I figure you used to live here, so you'd probably know. Have a favorite?"

She still seemed put out with him, but did answer. "One of my favorite places is very near here. At the end of the street, take a right. In two stoplights, head left. I will tell you when to stop."

Fair enough. He followed directions and found himself parallel parking in the middle of a little downtown district that had been revitalized with unique shops, antique stores, a cupcake bakery, and… "Primrose and Saxby's?"

Despite the rundown brick building, the lacy curtains screamed feminine and delicate. Carlotta sent him a coy smile as she approached the stained glass door.

Caleb pulled it open for her and a blast of sweet-smelling air hit him immediately. Flowers—and lots of them. Scented candles added another cloying note to the pungent, barfworthy fragrance. And *lots* of estrogen. Old-fashioned jewelry filled glass cases, framed by overflowing antiques that looked a hell of a lot like junk to him. And goddamn dolls everywhere in frilly dresses and dainty shoes with unblinking glass eyes. *Oh, hell.* What did women see in places like this?

A woman in a Victorian dress showed them to their table. A man in a tuxedo serenaded the crowd, singing sappy love songs and doing his best Barry White imitation. The menu consisted of items like chicken chutney salad, afternoon tea finger sandwiches, basil cheese tarts, and cream of leek soup. Carlotta pressed her lips together, looking exactly like the cat who swallowed the canary.

The waitress took their order, and he'd been thrilled to find a burger on the menu. Not his first choice, but the rest of this bird food would wear off in a couple of hours. Carlotta ordered a turkey swiss wrap and a lemon scone with clotted cream.

Caleb had no idea what that was precisely, but he had to admit that the food was actually pretty edible, even if the music made him want to vomit. She offered him half of the scone thing, which looked a bit like a hard turnover to him. He declined, and she bit into the scone. The look on her face as she did, the moan, the way she nibbled and licked her lips… Hell, did she have any idea how close he was to plucking her up from her chair, laying her across the table, and tearing her clothes off?

Gnashing his teeth as she spooned on some of that sweet white cream and finished the little dessert, he counted the minutes until he could escape this joint and get her alone.

"Did you used to come here a lot?" he asked to keep her talking. If they were having a conversation, they couldn't be fucking—at least in theory. He could think of a lot of things he'd like to say to her while buried deep.

A smile spread across her beautiful face. God, those plump lips he wanted to own with his own mouth, his cock, his…

Stop. He had to yank his head out of her pussy, at least figuratively. If he ever got there literally, he probably wouldn't come up for air for a long fucking while.

"Never," she admitted softly.

But she'd wanted to torture him a bit for forcing her to eat and make him regret bending her to his will. This place definitely wasn't his speed, but he wasn't going to wish he'd left her hungry.

"But I always wanted to come here. It looked…interesting."

Caleb frowned. "Then why didn't you?"

As soon as he asked the question, he knew the answer. Carlotta merely confirmed it.

"Gordon would say it is stupid to waste money on food I could cook better. He would say that the place is silly with its lace and dolls and the singer." She shrugged. "I would not want to come to such a place every day, but every so often would be nice."

And the ex-douche bag had been unwilling to bend for her, even just to make her happy. Caleb was more than glad he could fulfill this desire for her. He'd be glad to satisfy any other she might have, too.

He took a calculated risk and reached across the table for her hand. He heard her little indrawn breath when he curled his fingers around her. She tensed, but she didn't let go.

With a squeeze, he met her dark eyes. "Why did you stay with him for so long?"

"He put a roof over my children's heads and food in their bellies. I came to him with three kids. Whatever else I say about him, he provided for them."

"And treated you badly."

"I was not important. The children were."

Ah, damn… Her heart was so soft and sweet, and Gordon had taken advantage of it so badly that she feared trusting anyone again. Caleb knew damn well that he wasn't easy to get along with, but he'd never neglect or tear her down as Gordon had. He wondered if all her experience with love had been awful.

"Tell me about your first husband."

Carlotta looked surprised by his question, but happy for the change of subject. "Eduardo was a good husband and father. He was a police officer and died in the line of duty while breaking up a domestic dispute. The children were all young. I was a widow before thirty and a poor one at that. I had very much hoped that Gordon could fill all the voids in our lives, but…" She shrugged. "The nine years Eduardo and I shared together were lovely and wonderful. Even knowing how it would end, I would not change a thing. My children are the world to me, and I treasure my memories with their father."

And Caleb was actually glad to hear that. He just hoped that having something good in the past would help Carlotta believe that she could have something good in the future with someone else.

"You deserve to be protected and pampered, Lottie. You deserve someone who will be happy to indulge your whims every now and then just for the pleasure of seeing you smile. And you need someone willing to make sure you take care of yourself properly."

Carlotta seemed to hold her breath. She blinked at him. "I am too old now for matters of the heart. I have two beautiful grandsons and—"

"And if you finish that sentence, you won't like what comes next. You are *not* old." He gritted his teeth, his palm itching to meet her backside. Hell, he hadn't felt an urge to punish a woman this way in years… None of them had mattered enough to try. "Do you hear me, Lottie?"

"Caleb, stop. I know that I am no longer young. Once I was pretty, like my Kata."

"You're still so goddamn beautiful it makes me hurt to hear that you think otherwise. If you'd give me half a chance, I'd exhaust myself proving over and over how incredibly lovely I think you are."

A pretty rosy flush crept up her cheeks. "I am far too old for sex."

Caleb snorted. Is that what she thought? "Wanna bet? I guarantee you that I could make you think otherwise."

As soon as the words were out, Carlotta withdrew her fingers from his. He smothered a curse. Damn it, he was coming on really strong again, saying exactly what was on his mind, whether it would scare her or not.

If she was going to fall for him, didn't he have to be himself? Yes, but how could she get to know him if he constantly came on too strong and alarmed her?

Circular fucking argument. He had to play this cooler. The fact that he genuinely believed they could have something special shouldn't be a factor. Hunter had pushed Kata into marriage and nearly lost her. Caleb knew he had to be smarter.

Into her silence, he swallowed. "I'm sorry if I'm making you uncomfortable. I'm the kind of man who doesn't dance around the truth well. If there's something to be said, I say it. I've held this in for too long as it is. I'm sorry if I frightened you when I kissed you on our second date. I wanted you and I wasn't good about taking things slowly. I know Gordon hurt you. I didn't do so well with Amanda myself. But if you'll talk to me, share your concerns, I think we could…" *What? Ride off into the sunset? Live happily ever after? What were they supposed to do at this stage in their lives?* "Try again."

Her little hands curled inward to something nearly like fists, hiding her short red nails. "You scare me."

"I know. I'd be good to you, Lottie. Not perfect, but I'd do my best to make you smile."

She peered up at him with sharp brown eyes. "Do you really need my help with Hunter and Kata's house?"

"What do you think?" He laughed. "I admit that I used it as a bit of an excuse to spend time with you at first, but now that I've seen the place…"

"It does need a lot of work." She wrinkled her nose.

"A metric shit ton." He winced. Hell, he wasn't used to editing his language anymore. Amanda had always hated his swearing, thought it uncouth and crass.

Carlotta just laughed. "A colorful phrase, but you are right. You have your work cut out for you over the next few weeks. Somehow, I think getting back to my work as a surgical nurse will be a vacation compared to all that must be done before anyone can inhabit the house."

Absolutely true, but he was having trouble thinking much past her gorgeous mouth, that lovely, lilting Latina accent…and that tight sweater cupping her full breasts. Everything about her turned him on.

"Is that a yes?"

"Tell me about you and your wife," she said instead.

God, the request blindsided him. He didn't want to talk about that. What if he just confirmed all her worst suspicions with his explanations? But she'd been honest with him, damn it. He couldn't do less.

"We married too young. Neither of us were good at communicating. We both made too many assumptions." He dragged in a rough breath. "I grew up in a traditional—if loud—house with three brothers, two sisters, and lots of love. My dad was absolutely the head of the household, and his word was law. Everyone fought and laughed and roughhoused. Yelling meant nothing to us since we've always been a boisterous lot. Amanda didn't understand any of that. She grew up an only child—a surprise baby for very liberal forty-something parents. Her house was very quiet. No one ever yelled, well...except her when she wanted her way. Amanda learned early that through tears and emotional blackmail, she could rule the family. I can't fault her, exactly. She was a product of her environment, just as I was a product of mine. I proposed because she looked hot in a bikini. She married me because I looked good in a uniform. Looking back, we got together for all the wrong reasons. When I met her, I was away from home for the first time and I missed my family. I thought I'd just make my own. She just wanted excitement and to be swept off her feet. It didn't work so well when I was deployed more often than not and she had a baby on each hip and another on the way."

"So she was unhappy?"

To say the least. He nodded. "I tried the only way I knew how to take some of the responsibility off her shoulders when I was home by taking over. She resented me for coming in and arranging things the way I wanted before leaving again for months on end. I didn't understand that. She complained and cried. Drama didn't happen in my family. I didn't know how to adjust. I'd try harder, but not the way she wanted me to..." He raked a hand over his short hair. "I've matured and learned a lot since then. I won't say I'll never make the same mistakes again, but I will say that if I do, I'll genuinely listen and try to adjust. Did that tell you what you wanted to know?"

She cocked her head. "It did. Thank you. I had wondered..."

Yeah, he had, too, about her and Gordon, so he could understand. "So you're willing to try dating again?"

Carlotta bit her lip. "What will Kata and Hunter think? I would not wish to make them uncomfortable."

Caleb leaned across the table to her. "Our kids are grown, and I don't think we owe our futures to them. They're happy. Why shouldn't we try to be as well?"

"I see your point. Consider it a maybe," she murmured. "I will keep an open mind if you will try not to boss me around quite so much."

He'd try, but…no promises. His DNA just seemed wired to be Dominant. "Deal."

After he paid the check, he hustled her out of the restaurant and to the home improvement store. He grabbed a cart outside the door, noticing that her stare lingered on a little shop down the strip mall.

Caleb stood, stared at her, waited. Still, she only cast a longing look toward the shop's door, then averted her gaze with a fake, overly bright smile. The place wasn't familiar to him, but it seemed to be some sort of home décor store. And he didn't like her hiding her feelings from him.

"Would you like to go over there, Lottie? Maybe something there will be good for the kids."

She smiled faintly every time he called her that, and Caleb enjoyed doing whatever he could to make her happy.

"It is possible. I once enjoyed shopping there. Gordon thought it was silly and never allowed me—"

"Go." It would give him time to repress the urge to kill her ex-douche bag. "If you enjoy it and think it might help with our project, then I definitely want you to browse the place."

"I would not wish to waste our time when it is so short."

He'd stay up renovating all night to give her some time to visit the store if that was what she wanted.

"It's not a waste. Go."

"You do not mind?" She sent him a puzzled stare, clearly surprised.

"Of course not."

"You are not angry?"

Angry? Caleb didn't have to ask what sort of fucker she'd been married to. He'd heard plenty. He really wished he could meet Gordon in a dark alley and let the goddamn asshole be on the receiving end of some pain. Yes, he knew that the ex-douche bag hadn't hit Carlotta, but he'd been abusive in virtually every other way—stifling her, stripping her of her confidence and self-worth, making her feel small.

"Never. I asked you to decorate, so I'm not going to tell you how to do it or where to shop. I might remind you about the budget now and then, but this project is meant to make the kids feel more at home. If something in that shop works in their house, then go for it."

"Thank you, Caleb." Damn, her soft voice went straight to his dick. "How long do I have?"

They needed to get to work, and he knew it. But after years of her voice being smothered, he didn't have the heart to cut her too short. "Text me in thirty minutes. I should have retrieved the flooring by then. If you're done there, you can look at it and pick out the paint. We'll have to see what cabinets they have in stock and discuss what else we might need. How's that?"

Her smile could have lit up half his life. "Perfect."

Chapter 3

Thirty minutes later, Carlotta left the home décor store with a bag in hand. She clutched the plastic handles and smiled. It wasn't much, just pale gray-on-white placemats, a set of elegant wine glasses, a trio of white pillar candles with modern faceted crystal holders, and sepia-toned wall art she felt sure would be lovely in the dining room.

She sent Caleb a quick text that she was on her way over. He replied back that he'd meet her by the door. In less than two minutes, he stood there with a flatbed cart loaded with all kinds of flooring boxes and supplies, exactly as he had said he would.

Yes, he seemed the sort of man who would do as he had promised, but she had grown far too accustomed to Gordon, who had broken virtually every promise he had ever made to her, including their wedding vows.

Shoving the thought aside, she peered down at the cart. "Everything is ready, then?"

"Absolutely." He took the bag from her hand and carefully balanced it on top of all his other items. "I've seen the flooring. The hardwood is dark. They called it handscraped Brazilian cherry."

Carlotta clapped happily. "That will be lovely and warm. I can do a great deal with that. And the tile?"

"A ceramic that mimics the look of a gray-veined natural stone."

"I can work with that as well. Kata will enjoy those colors. Size?"

"There are a few here, some rectangular, some square, along with little one by one tiles. I'll need to ask Hunter what he was thinking."

"Probably a multiple-tile pattern. I will study them and figure it out. Do we know what cabinets are in stock yet? And the countertop options?"

"Come with me, Lottie." He turned and positioned the cart behind him, dragging it with one hand. The other he held out to her as he looked at her with those blue eyes that seemed to penetrate straight to her soul.

Her stomach knotted and danced, but she put her palm to his. He held her close, his grip strong but not confining. Would she find the man to be the same? Or would his strength turn overpowering?

They walked to the back of the store, and he quickly commanded the attention of someone who assisted them in selecting a configuration of cabinets among those in stock. Hunter and Kata preferred a more modern style, and these were perhaps a bit traditional, but with the right palette and accessories, she could make it all work. Countertops were thankfully much simpler. Carlotta didn't like the choices at the big-box store and knew a former coworker whose husband worked for a granite fabricator. A phone call later, he hooked them up with some remnants for half the price in a color that would accent the new kitchen in gorgeous fashion.

After arranging for the cabinets to be delivered the following day, they strolled to the paint department. She was surprised by how patient Caleb remained while she selected colors for nearly every room in the house so that each room would have its own identity but each room would blend together. She tried not to dither, but it was not a two-minute process.

While they waited to have the paint mixed, Caleb peeked into her bag from the home décor store. "Nice."

He pulled out one of the candleholders, so she reached in and withdrew a candle, balancing it on top. "I think they will provide a bit of everyday elegance."

Caleb sent her a considering stare. "I'm so glad you're here. I really would be lost without you."

Of course he meant the decorating…but at the thought that maybe he just might mean matters more personal, her foolish heart fluttered. Gorgeous, stable, educated, and attracted to her—in the few dates she'd gone on since her divorce, that seemed a tall order. Most men were bitter from ugly divorces, wanting a mother for their young children—or themselves—or still living with their parents and never been married with good reason.

"Why are you still single?" she blurted. Then she realized how rude that sounded and pulled back with an apology on her tongue.

He gripped her hand again, and this time used it to drag her against his body. "Curious about me, Lottie?"

"I-I just mean…you seem very, well…almost perfect. I cannot imagine that some woman seeking a man of such…" *Magnetism. Potent appeal. Sexual pull.* She settled on something far more benign. "Intelligence and kindness did not lure you away long ago."

"Nope. I haven't been all that interested." He dipped his head, his lips brushing her ear. "Until now. Do you have any idea how badly I want to kiss you?"

His words went straight to that place that no man had touched in years. Her womb clenched. She gasped, and a little smile fluttered over his face. "Caleb…"

His lips fluttered up her neck, a brushing tease. In the middle of a weekday, the store was virtually deserted. The employee from the paint department wasn't even facing them. There would be no one to see if she closed her eyes, puckered her lips, and lost herself in his sinful kiss that had once made her dizzy and flushed and wrought endless speculation about how skilled he would be in bed.

It was neither cautious nor smart, but Carlotta couldn't stop herself from tilting her face to his and letting her eyes slide shut. His lips didn't cover hers. Instead, a growl filled her ear as he plunged his fingers into her hair and tugged just forcefully enough that she couldn't call his grip gentle.

"You're tempting me, Lottie. Not here. Because once I start, I don't know when or if I'll stop. Think long and hard about that before you offer me your mouth again."

Then suddenly, he was gone—his fingers in her hair, his body heat against hers, that deep voice that made her shiver. She opened her eyes with fluttering lashes, then caught sight of his taut profile. Every muscle in his body looked tense, poised for battle…or sex. Her gaze flitted down. The front of his jeans protruded, looking even harder than the rest of him.

Instead of being scared as she'd been the last time he had kissed her, she felt herself tremble with excitement. Her belly flipped. Parts of her that she had barely thought of in years suddenly turned slick.

Goodness.

She turned away as Caleb took the cans of paint from the store's employee and loaded them on the flatbed. He rounded the square counter of the paint department, gathering tarps and paintbrushes, painter's tape and a bit of sandpaper. Caleb did not once look at her as he dragged the cart behind him, but her intuition told her that he was not angry. Rather, he was restraining himself. For her.

His actions were commendable and sweet. Still, she hoped that he would not remain too sweet.

Carlotta had never imagined that anyone—much less a hunk like Caleb—would find her attractive at this stage of her life. She felt a bit like pinching herself. Of course, his behavior suggested that he had always been attracted to her. Shortly after her divorce, however, she had been too anxious and shell-shocked to handle Caleb. She had wondered if he merely pitied her or thought she would be an easy mark to ply into bed. Over time and through Hunter, she had come to know Caleb much better and realized that he was exactly as he seemed: honest to a fault, steady, sexy. A protector. A provider.

A lover.

"Come with me, Lottie." His voice rumbled as he nearly sprinted to the checkout counter at the front of the store.

She rushed on her high heels to keep up and chastised herself for not wearing more practical shoes in a store this huge.

As they reached the register, Caleb threw everything on the counter that would fit and jogged to find another cart, shoving every item in the moment the cashier scanned it. Hunter had paid for the flooring in advance, so Caleb left that on the flatbed. He barely listened to the total the cashier rattled off, but swiped the debit card, checked his phone for the PIN, and punched it in. The second the machine spit out a receipt, he grabbed the scrap of paper and tore it free, tossed it in one of the bags, then ushered her to the cart. He took the flatbed with the flooring and jerked it behind him as he all but ran out of the store. He had the truck half loaded before she reached the parking lot.

Carlotta suppressed a smile. If he was half as aroused by the idea of a long, wet, hungry kiss as she was…then, yes, she was impatient to be out of the unromantic orange of the big-box store and to reach someplace more private.

On the drive back to the new house, Caleb remained intensely focused on the road. He gripped the steering wheel until his knuckles turned white. Thick silence shrouded the cab of the truck. Two yellow lights and a sharp turn into the driveway later, he brought his truck to a quick stop, then killed the engine. His abruptness startled her a bit.

"Out of the car, Lottie."

Suddenly, the swarm of butterflies in her stomach attacked. It was one thing to ponder kissing a man when she was desperately out of practice. After all, she had not kissed anyone since their second date. What happened if things heated beyond a kiss? She was not twenty-one anymore. Her body showed it. The thought of being naked in front of Caleb filled her with anxiety.

But no denying that she had missed having a man's touch. Being with Eduardo had been a rush of love, but short on actual pleasure. They had come to one another virgins, and the babies had come so quickly that they'd had very little time for satisfying sex. They had spent the next years being parents…and then a violent man had snuffed out Ed's life. Gordon had been her only other lover, and he had approached sex as he had everything else—selfishly.

She suspected that being with Caleb would be totally different. He might be a man of military precision, but he had the drive and ambition to be successful at any endeavor he undertook. The thought that he could give her true pleasure both excited and terrified her.

"Lottie?"

Whipping around toward his voice, she saw him standing at the passenger door of the truck, holding it open and watching her with a concerned expression.

She smiled and set her hand in his. Caleb gently tugged her down and against his body. He was hard all over, his eyes narrow as he studied her. His breathing fell in low pants on her face.

"Caleb?"

"Come with me," he said finally and pulled her away from the truck and up the walkway to the kids' new front door.

With a press of his key fob, he locked the vehicle. Carlotta looked over her shoulder as Caleb shoved the key in the lock and opened the door to the house.

"Are we leaving everything in the truck?"

Caleb pulled her into the house and shut the door, then backed her against the wall beside it. He settled every angle of his body to her soft curves and cupped her cheek. "I'm trying like hell to go slow and not scare you away again, but the way I want you…" He swallowed. "If you're going to say no, say it now, Lottie."

She drew in a shocked breath and blinked up at him. The way his fingers curled around her neck, the way those incredibly blue eyes delved deep into her, the desire tightening his face…he would not stop with a kiss.

The Catholic girl in her said that a good female did not have sex out of wedlock. The fifty-year-old woman whimpered that revealing herself to a man as fit and beautiful as Caleb would be nothing short of embarrassing. The hungry woman in her with thirty years of lackluster sex in her past wanted to know just this once what it meant to splinter apart because an experienced man had the patience and care to unravel her.

To hell with guilt and insecurity.

Caleb might be as subtle as a bulldozer and he might have frightened her once, but she had grown stronger, more confident. Today, he had proven himself competent of meaningful discussion. Over and over, he had shown her that he respected her fears and feelings. If things between them did not last and they still had to see one another at family gatherings…well, she would cross that bridge then.

"Caleb," she whispered, lacing her fingers around his neck, pressing herself closer to his body and the erection she couldn't possibly miss. "Kiss me."

Chapter 4

He did absolutely nothing for a long heartbeat, just tightened his grip on her and stared down into her face. Something primitive, possessive, snarled across his expression as he lowered his head with a moan and settled his lips over hers. Commandingly gentle. Trembling with tenderness. A brush, an exchange of breaths, once, twice.

Without a doubt, he held back for her, and the painstakingly polite kiss was touching—but completely frustrating.

In the past, all his heat and hunger had worried her. Now it just made her ache for more.

Carlotta tore her mouth from his. "Not like this, Caleb. Kiss me like you did the last time, when I felt certain you meant to consume me. So I can feel that you want all of me."

A feral smile crawled up his lips. "You don't have to ask me twice."

He pulled her away from the wall and into the middle of the great room, shrugging out of his jacket and laying it across the carpet.

"On there." He pointed.

She did not hesitate. In fact, the demanding tone she had once found intimidating now made a new ache dance between her legs.

Never taking her gaze from him, Carlotta eased down onto his leather jacket. It smelled of him, musky, so manly and leathery. Her heart started racing, beating in a mad rhythm. Her palms began to sweat. She had read such descriptions of women being excited by a man before, even heard a few whispers. She would have sworn they were all lies until now.

He attacked the buttons of his shirt as he kicked off his shoes and sent her a piercing stare. "Lottie, if you'd like to keep all those clothes in one piece, start removing them now. I've waited over two years for you. My patience has ended. I'll make it up to you later. Right now, I want you naked."

His words sent a shiver through her. Undress for him in broad daylight? She had never done that. Goodness, that sounded terribly sheltered. Her first husband had preferred darkness and they had rarely progressed past fumbling around clothing, especially after the children had been born. Gordon had often waited until she was asleep, frequently pushing her nightgown up and spreading her legs before she was even awake, much less excited.

"But…you will *see* me."

"Pardon my French, but I fucking hope so."

If anything, his impatience was climbing. He tore his shirt off his shoulders and tossed it on the ground. Carlotta's mouth went dry. Bulging shoulders, one covered in a faded, but still dangerous-looking dragon tattoo. A light dusting of hair just between rigid pectorals. They tapered into a washboard of abdominals that had her gaping in stunned silence.

"You are beautiful," she breathed.

"You are too, Lottie. I don't want to hear you try to tell me any differently. And you're stalling. Off with that blouse. I'd rather have your skirt off too, but if I have to just push it up and rip off your panties to get to you…"

He would. Caleb didn't even finish speaking the threat because he didn't have to. Carlotta did not doubt that he would follow through.

With a shaky nod, she reached blindly for the buttons on her blouse. No way was she taking her eyes off him. He was too beautiful. Besides, if he winced or turned away from the sight of her exposing herself…well, then she could cover herself again quickly.

Her fingers shook as she pushed each button through its opening. The cool air hit her collarbones, the swells of her breasts, her abdomen. Then Caleb was kneeling beside her, tearing the rest of it from her body.

The beige lace bra she had chosen this morning without any thought of sex was both sturdy and modest, and she wondered if he would be put off by something so utilitarian. "I am sorry it is not sexier. My…breasts are not small, and I am not as young as I once was."

"Not sexy?" He reached behind her, and with one hand, popped open the four hooks holding her bra closed. It slithered down her shoulders, and Caleb dragged it off her body, falling to his knees in front of her to palm one breast. "God, these are beautiful. You know you're never going to get me off of you again, right?"

It may have been the wrong reaction, but she laughed. It felt good to be wanted. It felt even better to be touched, and when his thumb flicked over her nipple, sensation zipped up her spine. She gasped.

"You have ten seconds to get that damn skirt off, Lottie, or I swear I won't be responsible for how fast I lift it or how hard I fuck you."

She peered up at him, then blinked, speechless. No man had ever used that language with her in the bedroom. Always, she had found that particular f-word a bit vulgar, but coming from Caleb's mouth with his growl of desire, it did crazy things to her heartbeat, heated her blood. She drew in a shaky breath...and realized that the seconds were ticking away.

His strong hands curled around her ankles. He took a moment to appreciate her one indulgence: red heels. The color of blood, about three inches high, they were sensible enough to be comfortable, but eye catching enough to be sexy. Then, one after the other, he peeled them away and tossed them to the other side of the room.

Their gazes met, clung. Her heart, which had beaten like a drum against her chest, stopped for a long second.

"Caleb..." She didn't even know what she was asking for. Reassurance? A promise that all would be well?

"I've got you. I'm going to take good care of you, baby. I'm going to make you feel so good. But get the damn skirt off. Now."

Something in that voice made her jump to obey, that steely tone of authority, she supposed. It wouldn't lie to her. It wouldn't let her down.

Carlotta reached behind her and unzipped her skirt. Slowly, she wriggled it down, conscious of Caleb's gaze roaming her. After three children, her abdomen was not as firm as it had once been. Stretch marks had faded to faint silvery lines long ago, but time and the years of idleness during her ankle injury meant that her midsection was no longer anything close to flat.

"Stop stalling, Lottie. I want to see you."

Finally, torn between being modest and being attractive, she lay on her back and pushed the skirt past her hips. The second it reached her knees, Caleb grabbed the black garment and tore it away, leaving her in nothing but a pair of lace-trimmed beige hipster panties.

He stared at her *there*, right between her thighs.

Carlotta groped for something to hold on to and found his arms on either side of her, holding himself up to hover over her. He swallowed, then bent to her, placing a kiss on her abdomen. It had to feel soft under his lips, but the lack of firmness didn't seem to deter him a bit. Instead, he moaned and kissed his way up, pausing to lave and suck at her nipples. The jolt of pleasure lit up her veins, sizzling over her skin. Back and forth he worshipped her nipples, one after the other, until they ached, took on a life of their own, and she arched to Caleb, whimpering.

"So beautiful, Lottie. So damn beautiful. That's it, baby." He cupped her breast as he sucked deeply.

Restlessly, she wriggled, squeezing her thighs together to combat the wet ache, but nothing worked. In her head, she knew that Caleb could see every flaw of her body in the golden sunlight pouring in from the windows across the room. But her body hardly cared. It soaked in his attention. It blossomed. It craved more.

She hooked her arms around his neck and dragged him up to her. His mouth fastened over hers, and it was not simple or gentle or measured. His tongue prowled inside, taking absolute possession. He kissed her as if he had every right to every part of her body and he intended to prove it. Dizziness left her in a shimmering haze of passion. It ignited, firing her desire to feel him deep. Thoughts fled. Insecurities silenced. Never had she wanted like this, never known such arousal existed.

Caleb came up with a gasp and wrenched away, balancing on his knees. "I left the damn condoms in the truck. But I'm clean and I've had a vasectomy."

She had never had to think about such things. She and Eduardo had let God determine how many children they conceived before his death. Gordon had never wanted children and had always worn a condom every single time.

"I… Yes. I understand."

"How long has it been for you, Lottie? I'm at the edge of my control, but I will *not* hurt you. I swear it."

"Almost four years," she whispered. "When I discovered that Gordon had been unfaithful, I told him that unless he would be faithful, I would not welcome him intimately."

Shock crossed Caleb's face, followed by determination. "I will do everything I can to make sure you never regret being with me."

Trust did not come easily for her, but Carlotta had no doubt he meant every word.

"Why are you still talking?" she whispered coyly.

"I'm not. And the only words I want to hear from you are about what feels good. And feel free to scream." He grinned.

Her belly tightened. Her folds not only hummed to life, but screamed with need.

Then he ripped her panties from her hips with big, urgent hands. She was still gasping when he pried her thighs open and cupped her mound with his huge, bare hand. His skin was hot, and his touch was a shock. Her back bowed and electricity raced down her thighs, then up again to settle under her slick, needy folds. Gently, he ground the heel of his palm against the most sensitive nerves. Sensations soared up, then up again, and up some more.

"So wet, Lottie." He parted her folds with his fingers, then toyed with that button of nerves, a gentle circle that had her mewling. "That feel good, baby? You want more?"

Blindly, she clutched at him and nodded, lifting her hips in supplication. Oh, he was going to give her an orgasm, and with so little effort. The promise of the pleasure just out of reach was a stunning, welcome surprise.

"Caleb!"

"That's it... Let it build. Let it feel so good. You're getting close, aren't you? Yeah. So damn hot, baby. Now look at me, Lottie. Right at me. I want to see your face when you—"

Her eyes flew open as the ecstasy rushed in, converging right between her legs, then exploded in a torrent of astonishing bliss that flooded her entire body. Her womb pulsed. Her body blazed. The power of it was enough to light up Mexico City. Long and breath stealing and amazing, the orgasm dazzled. His hot blue stare locked onto her eyes, taking her captive and refusing to let her go. Vaguely, she realized that she was screaming and her voice echoed through the empty house.

Then she was freefalling in the aftermath, but she need not have worried. Caleb was there to catch her, with his arms around her, pressing his lips to hers.

"God, that was beautiful, baby." His harsh, trembling whisper made her smile.

"It felt...like nothing I have ever known." She batted her lashes shyly, feeling rosy and damp and beautiful. "More?"

His blue stare pinned her in place. "No man has ever made you come with his hand?"

She blushed furiously and couldn't quite meet his stare. Hopefully, he would understand. "With his hand, his mouth, his…anything. Ever."

Chapter 5

"If I have my way, it won't be the last time," Caleb drawled.

Not by a long shot. Amazing that no man had ever managed to make her come. Well, on the other hand, maybe it wasn't. Not Gordon anyway. He was an asswipe of the first order, clearly. Anyone else she'd slept with didn't matter. If Caleb had his way, he would be her last lover—and her best. Because for him, she had been like a spark plug, firing quickly and powerfully. He wanted to see that again.

Caleb inched down her body, spreading kisses as he descended. Fuck, she smelled so good. Her arousal perfumed the air, and the olfactory high was making him dizzy. God knew it had made his cock steel hard long ago.

Then he reached between her legs, pried her open with his thumbs, and let his tongue drown in her sweetness. Carlotta gasped, clutching at his head.

"What are you...oh!"

"Tasting you, Lottie. I want you to come on my tongue."

She panted, writhing as he laved her clit, then sucked it into his mouth. "Men do this?"

Obviously not the men she'd been with. Had they all been fucktards in bed? Whatever... Corrupting her would be so much fun.

His blood surged at that thought, and he settled supine between her legs, putting one on each shoulder. Jesus, she was more intoxicating than a fifth of scotch. His body hummed as he sucked her clit into his mouth and soaked in her little cries. She thrashed under his mouth and his hands, totally lost to passion. She was stunning. Her heart might be guarded, but her body was wide open. Caleb hoped like hell that Carlotta letting him touch her flesh meant that he was beginning to earn her trust. Maybe after this, he'd get behind her walls, too—and closer to that heart.

"Caleb..." She arched as she panted his name. Her pussy gushed for him.

Yes, she was getting close again. He reveled in the sound and feel of her surrender. His tongue slid up between her slick folds, settling for a long moment just under her clit. Then he gave her a firm stroke of the little bud, concentrating on the hard tip that peeked out. Her breathing grew choppier. She grabbed for him with frantic fingers. Looking up the soft curves of her body, he lifted his gaze to her face. Their stares locked. Her melted chocolate eyes on him felt like a jerk of his cock. Damn it to hell, he wanted inside this woman. He wanted to slide so deep, stay there, and show her that was where he belonged.

Not once after Amanda had left him had he ever imagined making another woman his own. He hadn't wanted to. Now... This one wasn't getting away.

"Come for me, baby."

Her breathing stopped. Her entire body tightened and stiffened. He drove two fingers in her pussy and quickly found her most sensitive spot, rubbing in slow, firm circles. She gasped with a long, shocked intake of air. That spot against his fingers softened. Then her clit turned to stone under his tongue. And she screamed.

It was the hottest fucking sound he'd ever heard.

Her flavor slid over his tongue. So damn sweet. God, did she have any idea that he was going to chase her around this house for the next three days, trying to get his mouth on her pussy? Probably not, but she'd figure it out fast.

Shudders wracked her, crashing through her system over and over until her entire body relaxed. Now she was soft and sated. Now she would welcome him into her body.

Now he was going to stake his claim.

Caleb sat back on his knees and reached for his zipper. "You look so gorgeous laying there all flushed with your legs spread. Damn, baby..."

"It is immodest." She tried to sit up.

Gently, he pushed her back down. "Modesty has no place in bed with us. There's nothing polite about what I plan to do to you. And I want you to understand now that I don't intend to settle for the parts of you that you want to show me or that you think are nice. Right now, I want to fuck you. Hard. Then later, I'm going to love you so gently. But you're not going to hide or keep any part of your passion from me."

"Is this not just sex?"

He gritted his teeth. Is that what she thought? Why would he risk upsetting her or the family dynamic to get laid? "No, it's not.

I'm going to show you what this is."

Caleb tore open the snap of his jeans. His zipper hissed in the veritable silence. Her stare singed him. As he shoved his pants and boxer-briefs down and took his cock in hand, her eyes widened. She gasped. He grinned.

His phone rang.

Closing his eyes, he stared at the ceiling. The ringtone was Hunter's.

With a snarled curse, he pulled the device from his pocket and answered it. "What?"

"Wow, grouchy. And here I thought you'd be happy that I brought you some help. Kata got called into work for a few hours, so I dragged Deke and Tyler away from their cozy love nests. We should be there in less than five."

He opened his mouth to tell Hunter to go to hell for an hour, but Hunter had already hung up. Carlotta had apparently heard every word his son had said and gave a sharp sound of distress before hopping to her feet.

"Carlotta…" God, he was ready to beg her. And after seeing her body, it seemed a shame to cover it up.

Her hands fluttered. Panic held her eyes wide. She took one look at her ripped panties and her jaw dropped. Then she looked ready to kill him.

Fuck, the mood was gone.

Shoving his cock back in his jeans, he zipped up and stood. "This isn't over, Lottie. For now, go to the bathroom, and I'll bring you your suitcase. You can change there."

Palpable relief crossed her face. "Thank you."

She looked around for something to cover herself with, but he gathered her blouse, her skirt, her shoes, then pointed down the hall behind her with a grin. "Bathroom is that way."

Carlotta reached out for her clothes. Caleb shrugged and handed them to her. Even if she held them, she'd find it damn hard to cover her ass as she walked away. His smile widened.

"I will dress here."

"The windows are wide open."

As if realizing that anyone could look in and see her naked, she jumped away from them with a squeal and clutched her clothes tighter to her chest. Shame to cover up such a fine view, but he'd make certain to see it again.

"But if I walk down the hall naked, you will look at me."

"Damn straight. Get used to it, woman."

Carlotta tsked at him. "You are a wicked man."

"Oh, you have no idea. But I'll make sure you find out soon." He winked.

She rolled her dark eyes, but he saw a ghost of a smile playing at her lips as she turned away.

Caleb stared, watching as she made her way to the bathroom. She might have put a little extra sway into that sashay down the hall, but it confirmed what he knew. "Nice ass."

She darted into the bathroom and hid behind the door, then peeked around it and stuck her tongue out at him before slamming the door closed. He chuckled as he threw his shirt on over his head and fished the keys out of his pocket, happily plotting ways to kill his son.

After retrieving her suitcase from the truck and carrying it down the hall, he knocked, and she opened the door a fraction to grab it. She said nothing, but her dark eyes danced with mischief, promised more sensual delights…and maybe a bit of retribution for making her walk to the bathroom naked under his watchful gaze. Caleb looked forward to that.

She'd no more than shut herself in the bathroom again when someone pounded on the front door then opened it. With a whoop and stomping of feet, the solitude was broken.

"Dad?" Hunter called.

He dragged a hand over his hair, then took in a deep breath, reminding himself that responsible parents didn't eat their young. "Coming out."

Making his way down the hall, he found Hunter, his son-in-law, Deke, and family friend Tyler all standing in the great room, taking up most of the space—and staring at Carlotta's ripped panties on the floor.

Fuck! He winced as he bent to pick them up and shove them in his pocket. "When she comes out of the bathroom, not a fucking word. Not a laugh. Not a glance. Not a raised brow. Nothing. Do you understand me?"

"Tell me that isn't…" Hunter's jaw dropped. "You're fucking my mother-in-law?"

Caleb gritted his teeth. "I would have if you didn't have such impeccable goddamn timing."

Beside Hunter, Deke burst out laughing. Tyler followed. Hunter just swore.

"You told me to stop ogling her ass, so I did."

Hunter held up a hand. "I don't want to know what else you did or might do to her ass. Just...stop there."

"I wasn't in the mood to share. Trust me." Caleb sighed.

"What is she doing here?"

"She's decorating. I'll fix shit, but color palettes and throw pillows...not my thing. Since you've ruined the getting busy I had in mind, why don't you three go unload the truck. We've already been by the store and picked up most of the stuff we need to get started."

He tossed Deke the keys to his truck, and the big man caught them in one fist, then grinned. Tyler headed for the door with a chuckle.

His son-in-law slapped Hunter on the back. "Look on the bright side, man. Happy mother-in-law can equal some serious peace in your house. She won't be trying to run your show."

"She doesn't anyway."

Deke shrugged. "If Carlotta is happy, Kata will be happy. That can only be good for you, dude."

Hunter hesitated. "True. It's just a little weird. My dad and my mother-in-law..."

"Get used to it," Caleb growled.

Rearing back, Hunter blinked at him. "Are you fucking serious?"

"Back down, man." Deke tried to soothe Hunter.

"What? We don't get to be as happy as you and Kata?"

Hunter smiled wide. "It's not that. I just never thought you or Carlotta would get serious about anyone ever again. I'm just shocked. But it's a good shock."

Caleb let out the breath he hadn't realized he'd been holding. "Good. But if you didn't like it, that was going to be tough shit for you."

Tyler laughed out loud from the door. "This is every bit as entertaining as watching a toddler put his toy trucks down the toilet."

Deke marched over to Tyler and punched him in the shoulder. "Damn it. Last time Seth came for a playdate with my boy, he taught little Cal to shove his toys down the john, too."

That only made Tyler laugh more. "Just spreading the love one crapper at a time."

"Lord, what am I getting myself into with this whole parenthood idea?" Hunter asked.

"Your children will have lots of stellar influences." Caleb gestured to Deke and Tyler.

Suddenly, he sensed someone behind him and turned to find Carlotta in a soft pair of jeans and a red V-neck shirt that revealed enough hint of cleavage to fire his blood again.

"Hello, everyone."

Deke looked down, repressing a smile. "Hi, ma'am."

Tyler wasn't much more graceful, just more brazen as he waved. "Good day so far?"

Caleb wanted to elbow the troublemaker.

Hunter drew in a deep breath, then approached Carlotta with a gentle hug. "Thanks for your help with the house. I want to surprise Kata for Christmas." Then his son gestured toward him. "Don't let the big guy give you a hard time."

Carlotta just flushed. "What is first on our agenda?"

#

Two evenings later, Carlotta sighed with a smile. The entire house was looking largely transformed. With Tyler's and Deke's help, they had torn out the half wall in the foyer, removed all the old carpet, and peeled back the linoleum. Hunter had lent a hand until he had been forced to return to active duty, and Carlotta had seen the worry on her daughter's face as she'd watched her husband walk out the door, not knowing if he would return again. But Kata was strong—and she'd buried herself in work since Hunter's departure.

Carlotta looked around the kids' new house with a keen eye. Drywall had been repaired and the cracked window replaced. She had scrubbed the fireplace until the brick looked fresh. New paint had gone on every wall of the house under her watchful eye. The new carpet had gone in with the help of installers. The guys had laid the new hardwood floors and they gleamed in the space, adding new life and vibrancy. The cabinets were stacked in the kitchen and waiting for Deke and Tyler to return tomorrow to help. The fabricators would come measure for the countertops as soon as the cabinets were in place and had promised a quick turnaround. She had shopped earlier for new hardware for the kitchen cabinets, as well as the bathroom fixtures. Time had not been kind to the plastic faucets, and she had replaced them with something sturdier. Somewhere in the middle of everything, Caleb had found the time to mow the lawn, front and back.

He was an amazing man, and she could not deny that she liked him more with every moment they spent together. They had not, however, had another moment alone since that breath-stealing moment he had nearly seduced her on the living room floor.

Carlotta wished very much that Hunter and his friends had come just a bit later.

Across the kitchen, Caleb had removed his shirt and opened the windows. The dusk was surprisingly warm. Sweat sheened across his body as he lifted the cabinets across the new floor and set them in their place, rearranging them until they fit in the space.

"You okay, Lottie?" he asked.

Now that they were finally alone again, she wondered what might happen.

"Fine. I wish I did not have to go back to work tomorrow."

He snorted. "You'll get more sleep at home than you've been getting with Mari and her two kids."

As much as Carlotta loved her older daughter and her family, she couldn't deny that truth. She nodded. "Before I go, I would like to pick out the light fixtures so you can hang them. Oh, and the curtain rods."

He picked up a hammer from the floor and tossed it back in his toolbox. She gawked at every ripple of his body as he moved. So strong and male and... She sighed.

Caleb turned to her with a very knowing, very sexy grin. "Something on your mind?"

She hesitated. As much as she wanted to talk about what had nearly happened—or if she was honest, find out what the real deal would feel like—she merely smiled. No way would she let Caleb near her before she had showered. She smelled like paint and sweat and dirt. Not sexy.

"Dinner?"

With a nod, he stretched, reaching his big arms over his head.

Carlotta nearly swallowed her tongue. She really did not want to go back to East Texas alone, without knowing what Caleb felt like against her, deep inside her. But ladies never brought up sex. She bit her lip.

He just grinned at her. "Why don't you shower here? You brought a change of clothes, right?" When she nodded, he smoothed a hand over her hair, tucking a strand behind her ear. "Good. Get ready. I'll finish the prep here and shower. We'll grab some dinner and light fixtures, then come back and…talk."

Did he genuinely want to merely discuss things or was that code for sex? She had not dated in so long, and Caleb kept her tied up in so many knots, she was uncertain what to think.

But she merely nodded and got herself beneath a hot spray of water. An hour later, she walked out of the master bathroom all put together again with some minimal makeup and her clean hair flowing free. She had splurged on a bit of perfume and hoped that it made him want to be near her.

He stepped out of the bathroom down the hall, and a cloud of steam followed him. He looked beyond fine in a pair of jeans, a black T-shirt, some boots, and a sly grin.

"You look good enough to eat," he said in that low voice that seduced her.

Carlotta felt heat climbing up her cheeks. "You do, too."

"Hmm, how fast can we find dinner and shop? I can think of something else I'd rather turn on besides light fixtures."

The blood rushed up her face faster, but she edged closer to him. "Very quickly, I hope."

He tipped her chin up so she met his gaze. "I've tried to go slow and give you space and time to think. I need you to tell me if you're feeling afraid or worried."

"I am," she admitted. "But not enough to stay away from you."

Caleb wrapped strong, hot hands around her face and looked like he wanted to take possession of her lips. Then he gritted his teeth and stepped back. "Nope. If I kiss you now, we'll never make it out the door. We both need food." He took her hand. "Let's go."

She directed him to a small Italian place she had always loved. The wait was about an hour, so they put their name in and drove to the lighting store across the street. Keeping the tight budget in mind, she picked out new lighting for the kitchen, bathrooms, and dining room on sale. Caleb told the store owner he'd pick them up in the morning, then they headed back to the restaurant.

The hostess seated them right away, and Caleb ordered a nice bottle of wine. The lighting was low, the booths tall, the ambiance intimate.

He reached an arm around her and drew her closer. His very touch warmed her through and through—but his stare blistered her with need. She had not thought of intimacy with a man in years. Now, she could hardly think of anything else—or anyone but him.

The wine arrived, and the waiter poured them each a glass. She sipped hers with a little moan, then smiled at Caleb when his grip tightened around her. They quickly ordered before the waiter scampered off.

"What do you see happening between us?" he asked suddenly in a low voice.

Carlotta nearly choked. "Here is not the place to discuss that."

"That?" He raised a brow at her.

"You know…" She had been unable to drag her stare from his rugged face just moments ago. Now she could not meet his gaze at all. "Sex."

"So the sex we haven't had yet. That's all you see happening between us?"

"No. You may have guessed that I am not the sort of woman to sleep with a man without being serious or invested, and I know we have not discussed—"

"I love you."

His declaration knocked the air out of her lungs. Carlotta gaped at him.

He cursed under his breath. "I know blurting it isn't the most romantic thing, and I should probably move more slowly and let you think about this more. But I've been thinking about you since the night Hunter first took you from your ex-husband and brought you to me. I've watched over you since. I've wanted you since. And with every time I saw you, I got to know the tender-hearted woman under your scars. Don't tell me this is abrupt. I know how I feel."

Caleb wasn't the sort of man to fall in love a great deal; that went without saying. And she had not loved a man since Eduardo. She was very fond of Caleb, wanted him desperately, respected and liked him… "I am afraid of love. It sounds silly, I know. I never loved Gordon, and yet he still hurt me very much. But loving someone gives them power."

He brushed a knuckle down her cheek. "Trusting someone and giving yourself to them can also free you from that fear."

Her thoughts scrambled. He was right. "I never considered it that way."

"I think it's time you did, Lottie. I want to make you happy. But you have to let me try."

Her breath seized. She probably did love him, and that terrified part of her did not wish to admit it. But when her car had broken down in August, had she called the roadside assistance company she paid each year? No, she had called Caleb. Had she called an electrician when she had experienced problems with her circuit breaker? Or called a coworker to help her home after some outpatient surgery to help her ankle just before Halloween? In every case, she had leaned on Caleb, knowing full well that he would be there for her each and every time.

She licked her lips nervously, then sipped her wine. "You are right. I have been a coward."

Caleb cupped her face in his hand. "Not a coward, baby. Cautious. Understandably so. But you know I would never hurt you like Gordon did. I'm not married to my job anymore. I've learned a lot since my marriage. No matter what, I would never stop listening to you."

"I believe you." She met his deep blue stare and felt something in her chest give way, as if opening herself to the possibility of love with this man. She fell a bit more.

For a long while, she had wished she could have a do-over with her love life for the past twenty years. She had never imagined that her do-over would not be a rehashing of her past, but a brand-new future.

He pressed a lingering kiss to her lips. She heard him growl under his breath, then pull away. "You are dangerous to my restraint, baby. If I wasn't starving and didn't have a long drive back to Tyler to take you home, I'd suggest we skip dinner and…"

His long, slow smile made that little ache Caleb always incited between her legs grow to something more urgent and needy.

Before she could take him up on his wonderfully inappropriate offer, the waiter returned with their food. She dug into her lasagna, and he moaned into a plate of spaghetti. A bushy Christmas tree took up one corner of the room, its lights twinkling. Carols sung by Italian tenors hummed in the background. The holidays were supposed to be a time of peace, of being close to loved ones and celebrating all the joys in life. For the first time in years, Carlotta had a reason to celebrate that didn't have anything to do with her children.

Caleb made her feel alive again—young again. Needed…as a woman. Desired…as a lover. And yes, wicked. He made her feel very, very wicked.

Until him, she had not known how badly she needed that.

Between bites, he took a sip of wine, then turned to murmur in her ear. "I can't wait to have you naked again. Under me. Baby, I want to fill you up so deep. I can't wait to hear you pant my name as you grip every inch of my cock with your body."

She swallowed a lump of lasagna. With those words, a totally different hunger overtook her. Food could be reheated. The oven at the kids' house worked. In some ways, she felt as if she had been waiting decades to start living again. She didn't want to wait another minute.

"Can we leave now?"

He froze. "What are you saying?"

Carlotta clenched her fists, not sure how or if she could say this out loud. "We have known each other more than two years. We have waited, and now it feels like forever."

"And a day," he groaned and clasped her thigh in a strong grip, his hand edging up under her skirt, so close to her wetness that she gasped.

"Damn panties."

"You were not going to touch me here?" The idea shocked her—and aroused her.

"Oh, yeah, I was." He sighed. "But it's probably better if I don't. I want you to understand this is more than sex. I don't know exactly how much more, but I want to figure everything out with you."

"I want that, too." She smiled at him. Happy tears made her nose tingle and her eyes simmer.

"I wanted to make love to you for the first time on a bed, some place you could be comfortable. But with me staying at Deke and Kimber's, and you over at Mari's… Hotel?"

She wrinkled her nose. "Impersonal."

"Come back to my house with me. It will be a long drive to Tyler, but you don't know how many times I've fantasized about having you in my bed." Caleb kissed her neck.

Carlotta very much liked the idea of being with the strong man in his big bed, feeling like she belonged with him, beside him. To him. She could handle him now. She was stronger, and he understood. Caleb would not run over her and neglect her feelings as Gordon had.

"Yes," she breathed.

He pressed a hard, breathless kiss to her lips, then slid out of the booth. A moment later, he returned with two boxes and a receipt.

"Are you finished with your wine?" he asked as he scooped their dinner into the little Styrofoam containers.

"I do not care about it."

"Me, either. Let's go." He took her arm and tugged her from the booth. She tottered to her feet and let him usher her to the door.

"Well, if it isn't the ex-ball and chain," a terribly familiar voice drawled from behind her as they neared the exit.

Gordon. His voice dripped with reprisal. Carlotta froze.

She had not actually seen him since Hunter had carried her out his door. The little bit of speaking they had done had been conducted through attorneys. Now, standing mere feet in front of him, she could not bring herself to turn and face him and found the familiar anxiety knotting her up inside.

Carlotta dug her fingers into Caleb's arm, her mind racing, grasping for something to say to diffuse Gordon's anger. Then she paused. They were divorced. No longer did she owe him so much as a polite hello. No longer was she obligated to try to make his life comfortable or happy. She could waltz out the door without a word.

"We have nothing to say, Gordon." She tugged on Caleb's arm, urging him again toward the door.

He wasn't budging. In fact, she would probably have more luck moving a brick wall. Still, Carlotta tugged harder, before this confrontation turned ugly.

"Sure we do," Gordon corrected. "Or I do. Your hair is longer. It seems your clothes are sexier. But you're still fat. Does he know yet what a cold, uptight bitch you are?"

Her ex-husband wanted a fight, probably because she had left him and his dented pride could not tolerate it. After nearly fourteen years of marriage to the selfish bastard, she refused to give him anything he wanted ever again. Putting him in his place was not worth the heads that would turn or the tongues that would wag. He was not worth another moment of her time.

Carlotta pulled Caleb toward the door again. "Please, I want to leave."

He didn't listen. Instead, he tugged free of her grip and whirled on Gordon. Dread sliding through her veins like ice, she forced herself to face her ex-husband, too. He looked the same as always, short salt-and-pepper hair cut like a banker's. He stared up at Caleb with faded blue eyes, looking slightly panicked, as if he had finally realized that Caleb stood at least six inches taller and outweighed him by fifty pounds of muscle.

But she wasn't shocked when Gordon whipped out his bravado and flashed an insolent smirk.

Caleb stabbed a finger in Gordon's chest. "If you'd still like to be breathing in the next ten seconds, I suggest you shut your vile mouth before I squash you like a fucking bug."

She slapped a hand over her mouth and grabbed desperately at Caleb's sleeve with the other. He could not know the havoc Gordon was capable of dishing out, but she did—all too well. He would twist words and call in favors. He manipulated and lied like no other.

"Are you threatening me?" Gordon smiled as if he relished the idea.

His small ego and his small penis probably could not stand the idea that someone he found as contemptible as her had left him. That she had not pined and regretted her decision each and every day. That she had, in fact, landed someone more wonderful and manly. Not that he would ever admit that last bit, even to himself.

"I'm telling you the consequences of failing to shut up," Caleb replied. "Carlotta divorced you for being a cruel, neglectful, cheating douche. If you ever speak to her like that again, I will rip off your head and piss down your neck. I spent twenty-four years in the U.S. Army as a trained sniper. Want to try me?"

Gordon swallowed and paled a bit, looking pastier than usual. Then he ripped his gaze from Caleb's face to glare at her. "This one looks and sounds like the asshole who carted you out of my house like some damsel in distress. He was your son-in-law, right? So I'm guessing this Neanderthal is his father. You're fucking the family now?" Gordon shook his head. "I gave you a roof and raised your brats. After using you, this jackass will probably kill you in your sleep. Enjoy that."

Gordon bypassed Caleb and brushed past her before he darted out the door. Caleb flung the doors wide and stomped after him, a man on a mission with thunder in his eyes. But her ex-husband ran to his convertible and hopped in, peeling out of the parking lot before Caleb could catch him.

Carlotta rushed out the restaurant's door, balancing their leftover dinner cartons. She stopped short when she heard Caleb curse.

"The asshole got away."

Yes, and despite what Caleb thought, that was for the best.

"Let it go. He is not worth it."

He turned to her as if he suddenly didn't understand what language she was speaking. "There's no way I was going to let him or anyone else speak to you like that. Not ever, Lottie."

"I appreciate what you meant to do, Caleb. But I am a grown, capable woman. And I am fine. I did not need you to speak for me." She put a gentle hand on his arm.

"If you weren't going to stand up to him, then yes, you did. That's my role."

"He can only hurt me now if I let him. He was worth neither my anger nor my words. He wanted a confrontation. Why should I give him what he sought?" She blinked up at him, willing him to understand. "I know what sets Gordon off. Do not be surprised if he slashes his own tires, then calls the police to blame such a thing on you."

"I don't give a shit, Lottie. He treated you with terrible unkindness and disrespect. I won't have that."

"I would rather not listen to it. However, if it means keeping the peace, his insults, which no one else will hear, mean nothing to me."

"It means something to me. Pissant bullies like that only understand strength. Silence is weakness to them. He would have continued to browbeat you until he found just the way to make you feel every bit as miserable as he does. He's angry and jealous and determined to at least ruin our evening, if not ruin your life. I'll be damned if I'm going to let him."

"I would rather not give him the satisfaction either."

"So don't!"

"I am handling it in my way, and you took that choice from me without discussion. You silenced my voice, just in a different way than Gordon."

"Are you going to compare me to that asshole?"

Around them a family gave them a wide berth as they walked into the restaurant. A laughing couple in their twenties walked out with bright smiles, the woman wearing a Christmas sweatshirt that said, "BE NAUGHTY. SAVE SANTA THE TRIP." A nip was finally beginning to fill the air.

And standing here knowing that Caleb did not grasp her point of view—and worried that he might never—very nearly broke her heart.

"No. I will merely tell you that I do not need and will not have another man taking over my life. Will you drop me at Mari's house, please?" She walked toward his truck, clutching the Styrofoam and forcing herself not to look in his direction.

"I was going to take you home and—"

"I think it is best if we say good night." She drew in a shaking breath. "And good-bye."

Chapter 6
December 22 – Lafayette, Louisiana

Carlotta pulled up in front of Kata and Hunter's apartment and waved at her daughter, who stood on the balcony with a smile and gestured her inside.

The late afternoon sun blinded her as she exited her sedan and headed up the stairs. Kata popped back through the apartment and met her at the door with a hug.

"It's good to see you, Mamá. I'm so glad you're going to spend Christmas in Lafayette. Hunter is en route home now. I expect him in the middle of the night. Mari had Carlos take the boys to a movie, so she's been baking and waiting for you." She frowned. "It's Christmas and we're all going to be together. Why do you look so sad?"

She tried to paste on a bright smile for her daughter, but felt anything except happy. In fact, she had been unable to feel happy for nearly three weeks. "I am tired."

Kata only narrowed her eyes and dragged her to the sofa. "And I'm Santa Claus. Out with it."

"I do not wish to burden you."

"You're my mother, not a burden. You've always been there to help me with my problems. You kept me from making the biggest mistake of my life and divorcing Hunter. You raised me and loved me and...how can you think I'd ever do anything but listen and try to help?"

Carlotta fidgeted. Kata really should know something. On Christmas Eve, there would be a big surprise party at her new house. Kimber, Tara, and Delaney had all been planning it feverishly and keeping her apprised. Luc and Alyssa were catering from their restaurant, Bonheur. Everyone would be there...including Caleb. If she didn't tell Kata the truth now, her daughter would only ask later, when she should be focused on her new home and having her husband with her for the holidays.

She heaved a big sigh. "Caleb and I tried having a...relationship. It did not work, and I miss him far, far more than I imagined I would after such a short time."

Kata's eyes bulged. "He dumped you? That makes no sense. That man has been crazy about you—"

"No, *Mija*. I told him that such a relationship would not work. You and Hunter have settled your issues with control and power, and I know your…" She looked at the discreet collar around her daughter's neck, and after many conversations, understood what it represented. "Your private life has helped with that, but I—"

"Stop there, Mamá. Hunter and I have worked it out, and yes, understanding that his dominance isn't meant to flatten but *help* me has made a huge difference. I know the Colonel is a force to be reckoned with, but he would never make you miserable like Gordon."

"Not intentionally. He has a good heart. But he does not understand my need for independence, I fear. And to please him, I wonder…would I simply let him have his way?"

"There are so many things wrong with that statement…" She shook her head. "First, I don't think so, but *talk* to him! I don't understand… Tell me what happened—and don't leave anything out."

Trying to hold back her tears, she related the incident with Gordon at the restaurant. To others—maybe even to Kata—breaking a burgeoning relationship because she felt silenced may seem extreme. But after so many years of misery, she could not bear the risk of losing herself, of disappearing again. She would rather be alone and able to stand on her own two feet than to be utterly dependent again.

Kata leaned forward and took her hands. She hesitated for a long moment before she finally sent her an empathetic frown. "I understand. I struggled with so many of the things you're feeling now. I want to ask you a few questions and answer me very honestly, okay?"

"Of course."

"These won't be easy questions. First, do you believe in your heart that Caleb would ever want you subjugated and silenced? That he would disrespect or neglect you in any way?"

"No. He would mean well, always. He has a kind heart and good intentions. I know he merely meant to protect me from Gordon, but it is my battle to fight, *if* I choose to fight it. I did not. Gordon is a rat not worth my time and anger."

"But he's a rat who will come back if you don't put him in his place. Has he tried to contact you since you ran into him?" Kata sent her a knowing stare.

Carlotta flushed. "He called the hospital earlier this week, asking for me, and left a message."

"There you go. He believes that you're sufficiently cowed now because you didn't stand up for yourself. He may even believe that he can bully you into coming back. I don't know. But I don't think Caleb had the wrong idea exactly. Sure it might have been nice if he'd talked to you before he threatened the asshole, but honestly, what would you have thought of Caleb if he'd done nothing while Gordon denigrated you?"

The question ripped through her thoughts with quiet destruction. Carlotta had never considered the situation from that point of view. But she knew the answer immediately. "I do not think I could respect such a man. It reeks of cowardice."

"And that's something no one will ever accuse the Colonel of having. In his eyes, you were his to care for and protect. He wouldn't have been treating you properly if he had let Gordon walk all over you without saying a word in your defense. You know what would have happened if Hunter had been with you."

Yes, her son-in-law would likely have punched Gordon and threatened him with something violent and unrepeatable. By comparison, Caleb had been fairly restrained.

"If one of my ex-boyfriends ever treated me like that—"

"I would show him the sharp edge of my tongue immediately," Carlotta assured.

Kata smiled. "The instinct of a mother. I've heard you and Mari talk about it several times. You didn't even have to think about what you'd do. You simply knew. What about the instinct of a man in love? You think that's any less strong when men like Caleb are, by nature, protectors?"

Eduardo had loved her very much. He would have never let Gordon or anyone talk to her that way. Why should she imagine that Caleb would allow such a thing either?

Carlotta's thoughts tangled, and her head told her that Kata had some very valid points. Her frightened, half-frozen heart kept trying to override her logic, reminding her that her terrible past could repeat itself if she allowed something as foolish as hope to rule her.

"Kata, I…" But she didn't know how to finish that sentence because she did not know how to feel or what to say.

"Last question," her daughter assured. "You're very unhappy without Caleb now. I'm not even going to phrase that like a question because I can see you are. But you've avoided being with him because you're afraid to be unhappy?"

"Surely, this sadness will pass."

"But why should you feel it at all? When you were with him, before the incident with Gordon, were you happy?"

As brief as it had been… "Very."

Carlotta sniffled. Goodness, had she allowed herself to create her own misery?

"Do you really think after so many years with Gordon that you would fall back onto the same timid path or that Caleb would be interested in a woman he believed had no backbone?"

No, but… She couldn't quite find the right words to phrase her worries.

"You're scared." Kata summed it up. "I understand. Believe me, I *totally* get that."

With precious few words, Kata zeroed in on her issue. She was afraid of being back in that place, of being that person again.

"But do you realize that by being too afraid to move on and be with a wonderful man who loves you, you're letting Gordon win? Even two years later, even from a different state, even after the divorce, you're letting him dictate your life to you. You're giving him your power."

Kata's terribly honest words were a blow to the chest. A thousand thoughts all rushed her mind at once, the loudest that her daughter was right. If Gordon knew that he had stirred up enough fear to cause her to leave a man who genuinely wanted to cherish her, he would relish that. The small man would feel big. He would have the last laugh.

"I will not let him win." Carlotta clenched her fists, determined to get Gordon out of her life once and for all.

"I don't think you should." Kata hugged her and smiled. When she pulled back, her eyes danced with mischief. "You know…I think Caleb is due back in Lafayette tomorrow for the holiday. Maybe you should talk to him."

No maybe about it. She was no longer the timid woman whom

she had allowed Gordon to browbeat. She would not let him rule her life now. She would not remain unhappy because of him, not when Caleb was so wonderful to love.

"Thank you, *Mija*, for giving me a kick. I will."

#

On the pretext of visiting Mari and the boys, Carlotta left Kata's apartment and headed over to the new house. With only two days before Hunter would surprise Kata with this Christmas gift meant to cement their future, she had a lot to do to finish getting the house ready. Her trunk was packed full of gifts for everyone, as well as all the curtains, throw pillows, area rugs, and other accessories she would need to complete the rooms. Hunter would surprise Kata with a night in Dallas tomorrow, some "couple" time before the holiday started. Everyone else would move the furniture in so that when they returned for the party on Christmas Eve, their new home would be mostly complete.

And somewhere in the midst of all that chaos, she would pull Caleb aside, apologize, and ask if they could start over.

A happy little smile lit her face. Hopefully, everything would come together in her life this holiday season. Family, celebration, joy…and finally a man to love, one who not only made her feel cherished, but like a woman.

Navigating the last curve onto the right street, she arrived at Hunter and Kata's charming new house on the corner. The porch and trim had been painted, as had the detached garage out back. She frowned. But the door to the little building behind the house stood open. Had squatters barged their way in again?

Parking on the street as dusk gave way to night, she was grateful for the streetlamp that lit the path in front of her. She walked toward the garage carefully to investigate, clutching her phone. When she reached it and peeked into the darkened space, she didn't see anyone, just a familiar truck.

Caleb's.

He is here! Nerves suddenly fluttered in her stomach, and she drew in a shaky breath. It was probably a very adolescent reaction, but he often tied her up in so many knots that she behaved like that shy, uncertain girl again. When he kissed her though, all that slid away until she felt only flushed and needy and...like she was in the best hands possible.

Carlotta turned and darted back toward the porch, climbed the steps, then tested the front door. It was unlocked. The latch lifted in her hand. She stepped inside the house and gasped. Everything had been transformed—every surface painted or gleaming, all the light fixtures hung.

She wandered through the bedrooms and bathrooms, marveling at the new tile. Caleb had even replaced the vanity in the master bath with something that looked more custom and high end—and had double sinks. The frosted shower door with brass accents had been replaced with something sleek and frameless. The fiberglass tub had been torn out. A new clawfoot sat in its place. Caleb had done a magnificent job.

But she did not see the man himself. As lovely as everything looked, she yearned to see him, talk to him...touch him.

As she walked into the kitchen, the cabinets all fit perfectly, their countertops glossy and sleek. New appliances sat snugly in their appointed places, ready to cool and heat great food.

Suddenly, she heard a clink behind her and noticed the door ajar, leading to what he'd told her was the attic. A sigh followed, then a soft curse.

Caleb!

Grabbing the knob, she tore the door wide open and scrambled to the steps. Then insecurity hit her. What if his patience had run out? What if he had decided not to give her another chance? She nibbled her lip. She would convince him. She would do whatever she needed to prove that she was ready to move on, open up, and love him with all her heart.

She scampered up the wooden stairs, her heels clicking with each one. About halfway up, Caleb killed the light in the rest of the room and ambled into view. Shadows clung to his rugged face and bare chest as he blocked the top of the stairs. His gaze latched onto her, unreadable. Blue eyes could seem so cold, but never his. They were especially hot tonight, intense as he looked her over thoroughly.

"Lottie, what are you doing here?"

Carlotta didn't stop running, she merely reached the top of the stairs and launched herself at him, her skirt hiking up her thighs.

Caleb caught her with a grunt and held tight, so she wrapped her arms around his neck and pressed her lips to his with a little cry. He was damp with sweat and smelled like musk. Above the faint mustiness of the attic, the scent of leather hung in the air.

He staggered back a step or two until he had his balance again. But he didn't kiss her in return. Instead, he palmed her waist and set her on her feet, then anchored his hands on his hips. "What's this?"

"I was wrong and I am sorry. I refuse to let Gordon continue to dictate my life. You were trying to protect me, and I overreacted. And I love you, too."

Now that she had blurted everything straight from her heart and off her tongue, Caleb watched her in unblinking silence. The seconds ticked on. Anxiety knotted her up again.

She reached out, touched his bare shoulder, ridiculously relieved when he didn't pull away. With a caress over his taut skin, she reveled in his heat and hardness. "Caleb? Say something."

His lips pressed into a tense line. "What made you change your mind?"

"I missed you terribly, so much that it stunned me. I tried to shield my heart from you, close myself off, but you still managed to take up all the space inside. I talked to Kata earlier. She pointed out that I was letting my fear lead my actions, not my love. And my love is far bigger. Please tell me I am not too late."

Even the thought of this beautiful man turning away from her made her eyes swim with tears, her chest buckle. Every time he had tried to forge something with her, she had allowed her doubts and her fright to dictate her actions. She was still scared, but she would rather be brave and take a chance on being happy than be alone and trapped by her past.

"You've run out on me twice."

She had, and he must feel somewhere between angry and hurt, maybe even rejected. "Never again. I promise."

"I won't apologize for telling Gordon off."

"I would not want you to. I should have done it myself and saved you the trouble. I am strong enough to stand on my own two feet."

"I know that, Lottie."

"I want him to know it, too."

Caleb shrugged. "Who gives a shit what he thinks? But you

have to know that I'm always going to defend you. I'm always going to take care of you. I'm probably always going to be a little overbearing and overprotective. But it never means that I think you're incapable or that I want to suppress you, just that I refuse to see you suffer. Understand right now that I would never want to take away your identity like he did."

"I know. It was not you I failed to trust. It was me. It was my strength." She sidled closer and braced her palm against his whisker-roughened cheek. "It was my heart. But I have searched it now enough to know that it is yours."

Shadows grazed his strong cheekbones and the hollows around his eyes, making him look big and dark and dangerous. Carlotta's heart pounded as she waited for him to say something…

But Caleb only proved that he was a man of few words. He wrapped his arms around her and brought her crashing against his hard chest. Her head snapped back, and he swallowed her gasp as he covered her mouth with his own. Parting her lips, he surged inside, possessing her with a single kiss.

Carlotta stepped on her tiptoes to get closer, give him more, moaning as his hands roamed her back, pressing her in tightly, before he cupped her backside. Caleb fitted her directly against his male flesh, thick, hot, and erect against her moistening folds.

He ignited her as he rocked between her legs and fueled a fire so hot, only he could put it out. She wriggled against him, silently pleading.

Digging his hands into her hair, he tugged, pulling her head back. His lips hovered over hers. "Your heart is mine, you say? I want it, Lottie, along with the rest of you. I want to spend the night inside you."

Goodness, the way he talked to her…low and sexual, a deeply determined male not asking a question, but stating his intent.

"Yes," she breathed, spreading kisses over his jaw, down his neck. "Here?"

He hesitated. "How much do you trust me with your body?"

What sort of question was that? "Completely."

"Wait. Don't move." He pulled away and disappeared into the surrounding darkness, taking his body heat with him. She shivered, wrapping her arms around her. It was late December, and the temperature had dropped the last few weeks. It was chilly in the attic.

Then light suddenly flooded the space, and Carlotta looked over to see Caleb let go of the lone string beside the light bulb. The golden glow cast over his tense face. He squared his shoulders, looking suddenly taller, more…formidable. His piercing blue eyes looked through her remaining walls and seemed to see down to her soul. Carlotta met his gaze, trembling under all his silent demand.

"Take a look around us, Lottie. You know what this is?"

A padded bench of some sort sat just beside her. A seven-foot mirror dominated the back wall. A giant wooden X painted in red took up the rest of the space beside it. To her left, a rack of hooks suspended a variety of paddles, whips, and restraints. To her right, a bed with a massive headboard—and cuffs built right into the middle.

Her stomach dipped, rolled, and tangled in shock.

"I know. A dungeon."

She could not quite meet his gaze, but questions zipped through her head. Was he not just an alpha male, but a Dominant, like his sons? Did he want to use this equipment on her? How did she feel about the idea of being immobile and at his mercy? Her nipples peaked and the ache between her legs surged. She supposed that answered her question. Her body liked it a great deal…but what about her psyche?

"Are you scared about the idea of giving yourself to me here?" he asked. "I need your honesty, Lottie."

"A little. But probably not as much as you might imagine."

He raised his brows. "Not too scared to try?"

Carlotta swallowed. Her first thought was to ask him to wait until they were more established, until she felt more secure. But she was either with him or she was not. After many conversations with Kata about this topic, she understood the psychology of it. Caleb needed her to prove that she could put herself in his hands and give him all of herself because she trusted him. Because she loved him. And she needed to prove to herself that she was strong enough to handle a forceful man without losing herself. Together, they needed to form a bond through their communication and pleasure that would serve as the foundation for the "us" they would become.

Carlotta reached up and fumbled with the buttons of her blouse, slipping each one free until she slid the silky red garment over her shoulders. Then she shimmied out of her charcoal skirt and kicked it aside.

Finally, she stood before him, wearing only another serviceable bra, lace-trimmed panties, and her red shoes. "I am yours, Caleb. I will never be frightened by you again."

He sucked in a deep breath, his chest expanding as he stalked toward her with slow, measured steps until he stopped right in front of her, so close that the heat of his body radiated to her and made her shiver. "I haven't topped anyone in a very long time. I put this side of myself away because Amanda couldn't deal with it. But I can't pretend to be someone I'm not with you. It won't work, Lottie."

She understood that completely. "I know. I was never myself with Gordon. He did not want the real me."

"Just so we're clear, you won't be allowed to hide anything from me. If you're scared or worried or confused, you give that all to me, in or out of bed. Yes?"

"Yes." She dropped her gaze again.

He hooked a hand under her chin and made her meet his stare. "And I want to know what makes you happy, just like I need to know what makes you feel good. You spit it all out, the good and the bad."

She nibbled on her lower lip. "I will."

"You're going to find it hard sometimes, and I'm sure I'll have to dig it out of you every now and then." Finally, a smile cracked his face, and he looked at a little hanging flogger with a roguish gleam in his eyes. "But that could be fun, too."

She answered with a blushing little smile. "I always knew you were a wicked man."

His smile fell, and that compelling stare dominated again. "You're about to find out."

He ushered her to the bed, picked her up, and laid her across the sheets. She hissed at their coolness against her back, arching away from them. Caleb seized the opportunity, put his arms around her, and unhooked her bra. Her breasts sprang free as he tore it away, the chilly air beading her nipples even more. But his rapt stare suddenly made her feel hot all over.

"Give me your wrists," he demanded, his voice thick.

Trembling, she held them out to him.

Caleb took them in a firm grip and bent, dragging her arms over her head. Carlotta knew what was coming...knew it, yet the feel of those cuffs fastening around her wrists with a metallic click did crazy little things to her heartbeat. She gave an experimental tug. No way she was going anywhere. Her gaze bounced up to his harsh face, and she knew the mild panic sliding through her had to be showing in her expression.

"You're doing fine, Lottie. Deep breaths. Relax. Feel the softness of the bed under you," his voice coaxed. "Feel my hands soothing you."

He curled his fingers around her wrists, then caressed his way down her arms, all the way to where her shoulders lifted to stretch to the restraints. He swept his palm under her in a slow, soothing glide, feeling his way to her waist. His touch was so gentle, patient. As his skin kissed hers, he brought her to tingling life. She let out a long sigh of pleasure and closed her eyes, melting into the bed.

"That's it, baby. Just let go of whatever you're worried about. Give it over to me. I'll take care of everything."

She focused on doing exactly as he said, emptying her head, not dwelling on her less-than-pleasurable past experiences, not thinking about what he might demand of her next. She simply tried to put herself in his capable hands and trust. Even more tension eased from her muscles. She didn't even move except to let her lids flutter open when he bent to kiss between her breasts and pulled her underwear down her thighs, then off.

Caleb sat back on his heels. "Gorgeous, baby. Just perfect.

Running a finger from her cleavage, down her abdomen, all the way to her slick folds, he stared, cataloging her every reaction. He watched her breathe, blink, flush. And he smiled.

"Are you happy?" She wanted to know, *had* to know, if he was pleased by the sight of her naked and bound for him.

"You have no idea. Having you here fills a need that's been gaping inside me since we met, but you surrendering this way… You can't know how much I've longed for the right woman to submit to me. I have no doubt now that you are that woman. Lottie…"

Whatever he had planned to say dissolved as he eased on top of her, balancing himself on his elbows—with his mouth right over her nipples. He breathed on them, a hot, toe-curling pant. She felt him all the way through her body and tried to arch again. The hard tips brushed his lips, and Caleb's gaze scolded her for rushing him, but he licked one of the tender buds. She gasped. They had become so rigid and far more sensitive than she could ever remember.

When he sucked her nipple deep into his mouth, she moaned his name.

"These are beautiful, baby. I'm going to want my mouth on them a lot. You'll see."

That sounded like heaven.

He repeated the process with her other nipple, suckling her so slowly, she wanted to throw her arms around him and scratch his back, force his head farther onto her breast—something. The cuffs assured she could do nothing but take the slow climb of arousal he dished out.

And Caleb dragged it out, forcing her to wait, to take the pleasure until she was restless and writhing under him. Then he stood and shucked his jeans and boxer-briefs, exposing the rest of his lean, sculpted body, along with that large, jutting masculine flesh she prayed would fill her soon. *Dios*, he was beautiful.

He wrapped his hand around his staff and caressed it slowly with a slight turn of his wrist as he neared the tip. As he threw back his head and hissed, Carlotta felt her mouth water and thought she might go insane if he didn't do something soon.

"I need…" She panted, trying to catch her breath and keep her wits.

"Tell me, Lottie." He continued with that maddening stroke up and down his erection, teasing her, toying with her wishes until they became desperate.

"I need you inside me. I need to feel you deep. I need to feel like yours."

Caleb climbed back on the bed and settled himself between her legs as he spread them wide, his gaze roaming her well-loved nipples, her soft belly…her slick flesh that ached for him.

"I'm going to thrust inside you and I'm going to fuck you deep, baby. You're going to know you're mine." He grinned. "But if, after that, you're still not totally convinced, we can do it again."

Lightness and a ridiculous overflowing of joy filled her. "I might need a lot of convincing."

"My pleasure. Let's see if we can give you some, too."

He clamped hot hands around her thighs, electrifying her with his touch. Her body jolted.

"Shh," he soothed. "I've got you."

Yes, he did, and she gratefully let his palms drift up, until his seeking fingers prowled through the slick flesh between her legs and he rubbed slowly at the bundle of nerves there. She wanted more of the orgasms she knew Caleb was capable of giving her, but she also wanted to join with him so very much…

"Please," she whimpered.

"Let it build a bit, Lottie. Trust me to know what to do."

She didn't even have to answer. He proved very quickly that he knew exactly how to arouse her. His teasing fingers plied over her little button and the pleasure clawed through her body until she arched and wailed and spread her legs wider.

"Pleeeaaassseee…"

"I like to hear your begging. Soon. Really soon, I promise. God, your pussy is so pretty, all deeply rosy and pouting. And so wet. I know you're going to be tight. You're going to kill my self-control. I've waited forever for you, and I'll be damned if I'm not going to make sure you enjoy this."

"I will," she swore, all but begging. "I am sure. Whatever you want…"

Caleb chuckled. "Exactly what I wanted to hear."

Before she could reply, he slid two of his fingers on either side of her bundle of nerves, creating a new sensation, exciting her with a whole new friction. Her breathing hitched, and she clenched her hands into fists. Frantically, she lifted her hips to him.

He pushed them back down. "You can't make me give this to you any faster. A little at a time. Let it burn slow, baby."

"It is so…overwhelming. The burn, it almost hurts."

"What hurts is the prolonged wait. Have you thought about me in the last few weeks?"

She nodded desperately. "Every day."

"Every night?"

"Yes."

"Did you want to call me?"

Goodness, more than he knew. "Many times."

"Did you miss me?"

"Every moment."

"Did you want me in your bed? In your pussy?"

No man had ever spoken to her this way, and she found it aroused her unbearably. "Constantly."

"Did you touch yourself and think of me?"

She flushed. How could she be honest about that?

He pulled his hand away, ceased that constant, sweet stroke on her most sensitive flesh. "Lottie, I asked you a question."

The burn turned hotter, hurt more.

"Yes." She felt as if the word had been wrenched from her soul.

He resumed stroking her, this time a bit faster, as if in reward. "Did you come?"

"Yes…" she whispered.

"I jacked off every goddamn day thinking of you. I came to Lafayette tonight because I knew you would be here. I'd planned to finish putting together the dungeon, then shower up and head to the kids' apartment. We were going to have dinner and talk, then I was going to take you somewhere—anywhere—and fuck you until you admitted that you were mine."

"I am yours. I said it earlier. I say it again now." She twisted her head from side to side, her voice a high-pitched pleading. "I will say it tomorrow and every day you will listen. Please!"

He eased down to her side, his fingers never leaving her except to slide two inside her and part them wide while his thumb rubbed her clitoris. The sensations were even more dazzling, and she felt the rush of orgasm begin to gather between her thighs, the bliss flooding her body. Every muscle tensed. She held her breath.

And Caleb covered her with his body, gathered her thighs in his grip, and probed at her entrance…

#

Finally.

Carlotta Buckley was about to become *his* after weeks and months of waiting and hoping and wanting. His—now and always.

He drove his cock inside her in one smooth stroke, pushing past clamping, fluttering muscles so tight with need.

The head of his dick scraped her soft, silken walls, and he groaned low in his chest. *Jesus!* There was no way he was going to last long, especially when she gasped and moved with him, urging him deeper. He slid all the way down into her. *Like fucking molasses.* She gripped him as he withdrew, then shoved his way inside her again. If anything, she was more snug, her body even more poised on the edge. *So goddamn perfect.*

"We're going to come together, Lottie. I can feel you, baby. I know you're close. But you wait for me, you hear?"

She threw her head back with a whimper. But she nodded. God, Carlotta in the throes and impaled on his cock was even more beautiful than he'd imagined. Sensual. Sexual. Womanly. She fucking glowed, and he wanted the chance to do this to her every day for the rest of their lives.

"That's good," he praised, picking up his pace. "So good…"

Every movement tingled up his spine. Blood surged through his body as he pumped her deeper, faster, harder. Hell, she was going to blow the top of his head off. That snug little pussy clamped down on him again. She moaned once more, cried out his name.

Caleb was done for.

He adjusted her thighs into the crooks of his elbows and slammed his mouth over hers. She whimpered again as he kissed her. Her tongue danced an uninhibited tango with his as he pounded her cunt, one deep stroke after the next. Then that unmistakable thrill zipped down his spine. Tingles brewed in his balls. His cock blazed with need, and he felt everything rising up inside him.

"Now, Lottie. Come!"

She surrendered the rigid hold she'd held over her body, and her flesh gripped him unmercifully before pulsing all around him, stroking his cock. His eyes closed as the ecstasy steamrolled him, and he groaned as he spilled deep inside her, feeling her buck and jolt, yet somehow moving with him as she screamed.

After a long, hazy moment, the orgasm subsided, and he felt Lottie's mouth still under his. The passionate fucking gave way to a deep kiss of reverence. Then he lifted his head.

"You're mine now."

"Yours." She smiled up at him, tears shimmering in her eyes. "I feel so…cherished and beautiful. Thank you."

"Don't thank me, Lottie. Love me."

She pressed a soft kiss to his lips. "I do. I think I always have. I know I always will."

Chapter 7
Christmas Eve

Carlotta stomped on her breaks in front of Gordon's house, and the car came to a shuddering halt as the morning sun streamed through the windshield. She had long ago ceased thinking of this as their house. Her time here in this prison had passed. As she looked out the window at the wide, perfectly manicured lawn and big beige front door, a thousand unhappy memories assaulted her. How had she lived here, so stifled, for so long?

"You don't have to do this," Caleb said beside her from the passenger's seat. "If you choose not to, it won't change who you are, my opinion of you, or what happens next with us."

She turned to him. Other than her children, he was the brightest spot in her life. She had awakened this morning with a smile, wrapped in his arms. Slowly, he had caressed her well-loved body, arousing it, then filling it again. And she thanked God for giving her this man and this second chance at a happy future.

"Thank you, *querido*. But I need this. For me."

He peered up at the house and through the window. "I don't see a tree up. Are you sure he's going to be home?"

"Gordon does not like Christmas trees. In his opinion, they are silly and messy, even artificial ones."

And she thought about all the years that she did without or made do with an artificial tabletop shrub wrapped with tinsel and a few bulbs for the children's sake. Since leaving Gordon, she had put up a lavish tree for herself each year, just because she could. And the huge, beautiful tree that she and Caleb had decorated in Hunter and Kata's new house would take everyone's breath away. It had certainly stolen hers...along with the deep kisses of passion Caleb had given her as they decorated.

"Gordon will be here," she added. "He does not work on Christmas Eve and does not speak to his brother, which is the last of his family."

"Definitely a miserable prick," Caleb commented.

His face asked how she could have stayed married to such a jerk for so long. Carlotta knew that if she had to do it all again, she would find some other way to support her children. Go back to school, pound the pavement for a better job. She might have taken the help that Eduardo's parents had offered after his death. Then she'd been too scared and proud and worried that his wealthy, influential family would take the children from her. Those fears had largely been in her head, and because she had been too frightened to ask questions, she had withdrawn into herself—and made an easy mark for Gordon.

No more stalling. She wanted to start this holiday season with a lighter load, a brighter future. Time to jettison the past.

"I will be back shortly." She opened the car door.

Before she could step out, Caleb put a firm hand on her arm. "So long as we understand one another. You do not go in the house and allow him to shut the door behind you. You don't place yourself at his dubious mercy."

Carlotta nodded. They had talked about how to keep this confrontation safe. He didn't like that she needed to do this, but he respected it. She leaned forward to kiss him. "He will not lay a hand on me. I will not allow him to put me in a vulnerable position. I will be back in two minutes."

He nodded, the strong angles of his face tight. "And I'll be watching."

With a little smile, she stepped from the car and shut the door behind her. Yes, she might have been motivated to do this eventually, but Caleb…wonderful, solid Caleb, had given her the strength to both see that she needed to exorcise this part of her past and the will to do it.

Up the long curved walkway, Carlotta found her stomach tangling into knots. The familiar hollow feeling emptied out her chest. *One foot in front of the other.* Breathing was difficult as she knocked on the door.

Gordon answered a minute later in a pair of slouchy sweat pants and a dingy undershirt. His grouch expression morphed into something curious, almost gloating, when he caught sight of her.

Leaning against the portal, he smirked. "Seen the error of your ways finally? Did Kata's father-in-law see how worthless you are, too? Did he kick you to the curb? Aww, and on Christmas Eve."

"No, Gordon. For once, you are not dictating the conversation. I am, and you will listen to me. I never want to see you again. Stop calling my place of work. If you happen to see me in public, ignore me. I will do the same to you. Nothing that comes out of your vile mouth is of interest to me. You have never respected me in the past, but I am demanding you to respect these wishes."

"Why? For the sake of our fabulous years of marriage?" he sneered.

"I would like to say because you are a decent human being with a heart, but since I know better, I will instead tell you that you no longer have the power to hurt me. Once, I may have been made of glass and you might have broken me into little pieces at will. Now, I refuse to let you crush me. You will never see my shards again."

"Pretty speech, bitch. But I don't believe it. You're still the same pathetic woman who hobbled around my kitchen and clung to me the second I walked in the door every night." He glared. "So, did that big asshole you were with when I last saw you tell you how much he values you and what a beautiful woman you are so that he could fuck you? Did you believe him? Are you feeling all strong and mighty now that he pumped you up to pump his way inside you, you stupid whore?"

His contempt angered Carlotta, but it didn't hurt her. Gordon was like a child lashing out because someone else wanted the toy he had cast aside. *He* couldn't hurt her, not ever again. "No. Caleb knows how to love. He knows how to be a true partner. He would never tear me down to build himself up. Of course, I am certain that was simply your way of compensating for your very tiny penis. But I no longer care. I will not say good-bye, Gordon. I wish you nothing well. Instead, I think I will leave you with a very cheerful fuck off."

She had never uttered that word in her life, and saying it now felt so damn good. So freeing. She smiled as she turned to leave.

Gordon grabbed her by the arm and yanked her back. With a terrible snarl and wide, maniacal eyes, he curled his arm around the front of his body, like he meant to backhand her across the face. Fear surged. Carlotta tried to tug herself free, but could not budge his grip. Instead, she kicked, hitting him in the shin, earning a nasty curse from him. But he gripped her tighter.

"Take your hand off of her right this fucking second or I'll do this world a favor and take you out," Caleb growled behind her.

Instantly, Gordon let go. Then he shoved her away, smirking when she stumbled.

Caleb caught her, then turned her to face him. The familiar

comfort of his blue eyes, his searching gaze full of concern, set her at ease. "I am fine."

He kissed her forehead. "Go to the car, Lottie."

"Let us go together. I have nothing more to say to this scum."

"I do." His jaw tightened. "Wait in the car."

"But I have said my piece."

"I haven't. Gordon and I need to be crystal clear, baby. Go on."

Careful, she mouthed to him. He nodded and sent her off with a guiding hand at the small of her back.

Carlotta did not like leaving Caleb with Gordon. Not that she thought her man incapable of defending himself against the weasel. More that she worried Caleb would not see Gordon's sneaky manipulation until it was too late. But he had respected her need to speak her mind. She could allow him no less.

In the car, she waited, wringing her hands, watching with an unblinking gaze. They exchanged some low, heated words—nothing she could hear. Suddenly, Gordon paled and stepped back. Caleb smiled, gave him the one-fingered salute, and marched back to the car.

When he hopped in, she stared, mouth agape. "What did you say to him?"

Caleb just grinned, supremely satisfied. "Let's just say he understands now that if he bothers you again he'll have a sniper, two SEALs, a former Army Ranger, and a former CIA operative willing to end his miserable life and hide the body so it will never be identified. I might have described just a bit how that could happen. Just for a minute. Nothing too over the top."

Carlotta thought she should probably be horrified or maybe even angry that it had taken Caleb's threat to make Gordon understand. But she wasn't going to change the little bastard. The important thing was that she had changed herself. And even when she had not let Caleb hold her hand for every part of this journey, he had been with her in spirit, showing her from the beginning what a true man should be.

"You really are a wicked, wonderful man."

#

Later that evening, Caleb sneaked a kiss as Carlotta put the last of the accessories in place. For the last two hours, she'd been running from room to room, checking drapes, fluffing pillows, straightening out area rugs, flipping on lights…

"It looks perfect, baby. You've done a terrific job. Come have a glass of wine and enjoy how great the house looks before everyone arrives."

Earlier in the day, Tyler, Deke, Jack, and Logan, who had just gotten leave, brought over all Hunter and Kata's furniture, setting it perfectly in place. Carlotta had packed a few of their clothes and essentials into boxes and brought them over as well. Kata and Hunter would no doubt move the rest out of their old apartment. But everything in the house now looked fresh and organized and like something out of a magazine—a far cry from the house they'd walked into a few weeks ago.

"Everything you did to the house, *querido*, made it a much better place to live. I merely added color."

"Along with a lot of love."

He hugged her tight as Logan shoved open the front door, holding Tara's hand. They both looked around the house with big smiles, stopping in front of the towering Christmas tree decorated entirely in red and gold, a shimmering jewel in an otherwise sleek great room.

Caleb approached his younger son and clapped him on the back. "Good to see you."

"Hey, Dad." He turned, and they bumped shoulders.

Then Caleb broke away and leaned over to Tara. As always, she was such a tiny thing, and he was careful as he wrapped her in a gentle hug.

"Everything looks great," Logan's wife said with a wondrous smile. "Hi, Carlotta."

She bustled forward, looking sexy as hell in a black V-neck sweater with gold flecks, a short black skirt that showed off those legs he'd become addicted to getting between. It hugged her luscious ass…and damn, he'd better stop this train of thought or he'd be sporting a hard-on when the party started.

After Carlotta hugged both Logan and Tara warmly, his son's wife handed Lottie some of the drinks they'd brought for the party. The two women immediately went to the kitchen to chill the cans and bottles.

Logan sent him a speculative glance. "Still just looking at Carlotta?"

"Nope." He grinned widely.

His son laughed. "I kind of got that impression. I wasn't sure if we were going to have to leave the room quickly because you sure looked like you wanted to undress her right that instant."

"I did. I still do. But I can wait. At least five minutes."

"That long?" Logan drawled, then he laughed. "Good for you, Dad. I hope you two will be really happy."

"I think we will. Time will tell, right?" He shrugged. "What about you? How long is your leave?"

Logan's smile fell. "A few days. I've been promised a longer one in the spring. In the meantime, I've talked to Hunter. He's going to let Tara stay here with Kata while I'm on active duty, and it's a huge relief to me to know she'll be with family, just in case."

"That's great. It's perfect."

"Almost. Yeah…"

Before Caleb could question his son on that comment, Kimber clattered in on a pair of towering black heels, carrying bags of chips and a couple of bowls of dip. Behind her, Deke entered with their son, Cal, balanced on one hip. He held a twelve-pack of beer in his free hand.

Cal lunged out of Deke's arms to reach Caleb, and he grabbed his growing grandson, tossing him in the air just to hear the little boy giggle.

Kimber kissed his cheek, and Caleb marveled again at how beautiful she'd grown and how happy she looked. Never in a billion years would he have thought she and Deke would be good for one another, but they'd both seemed to flourish, their love almost a tangible thing.

"Good to see you, Dad."

"You, too, little girl." He smiled at his only daughter and tickled Cal again.

Deke paused behind his wife. "Kitten, am I icing the beer down in the kitchen?"

"Probably. Let's go see."

"Carlotta and Tara are in there, likely organizing everything to perfection."

"Great. I'll go join the estrogen party." Kimber laughed.

Deke shuddered. "I'll, um…stay out here and admire the Christmas tree. Damn, this place looks great. Much better than the day Tyler and I first walked in."

Caleb nodded. "It was a lot of hard work, but worth it."

The door opened again before Deke could reply. Tyler shouldered his way in. His son Seth started wriggling uncontrollably when he spotted Cal.

"Down," Caleb's grandson demanded, so he set the boy on his feet.

He skipped over to Seth and the two immediately took up with some stuffed trucks that Tyler handed down to the boys.

Tyler's wife, Delaney, blew in with a little shiver a moment later, stripping off her coat to reveal her swelling belly under a lovely deep green dress. Seth was not quite two and would have a brother or sister to love shortly after his birthday.

With an indulgent grin, Tyler took her coat and draped it over the back of the sofa, then settled a hand over her belly. "Active tonight?"

"Yeah, our little sweet pea must know there's a party." Del laughed.

Logan tripped out from the kitchen and shook both Deke's and Tyler's hands, then looked at Del's coat with a frown. "It's not that cold."

"According to you," she returned. "Remember me? Thin Southern California blood here."

They all had a laugh, and Delaney kissed Tyler before she drifted to the kitchen to join the other ladies. Her wedding ring winked on her left hand under the gleam of the recessed lighting. Their wedding had been rushed with another baby on the way, but it had been an intimate, joyous event shared by this close-knit bunch a few months ago.

The doorbell sounded a moment later, and Tyler turned to open the door. Jack Cole stepped in and greeted the other man with a hearty handshake. He had a blue diaper bag with soccer balls and teddy bears draped over his shoulder, and Caleb shook his head. He'd never thought he'd see the day when big bad Jack toted baby crap around and doted on a gorgeous redhead. Morgan Cole came in behind her husband, looking as lovely as always in a frilly black dress and showing a lot of cleavage. Their sleeping son, just a few months old, rested on a burp cloth laying over her shoulder.

Jack turned to take the baby from her and glowered at the amount of cleavage the dress showed.

"Jack, it's not like I can help it. When I'm breastfeeding, boobs happen."

"And only I'm supposed to see them," he growled. "Remember that." He pulled gently at the lavish ruby collar around her neck.

"You're such a caveman." She rolled her eyes, but the indulgent smile said that she didn't mind his possessiveness a bit.

Caleb repressed a smile and headed toward the couple. "Hi, Jack. You look fabulous, Morgan. Really happy."

"Thank you. Life is perfect today. My brother, Brandon, called me earlier. He and his girlfriend, Emberlin, got engaged last weekend. They're going to come see us for New Year's. You're looking great yourself."

He smiled. "Motherhood seems to agree with you."

"Brice is an angel." She grinned with so much pride at the infant in her husband's arms. "He's a great sleeper and a great eater."

"And really great at wailing for his mom whenever dad thinks he might get lucky."

Around Jack, most of the men laughed. Caleb nodded. "I remember those days…"

"Tell me they end soon," Jack nearly begged.

"Sure," Caleb quipped. "In about eighteen years."

He covered baby Brice's ears. "Fuck off, Colonel."

"Same to you." He laughed. "Beer's in the kitchen.

"Thank god!" Jack turned to his wife. "You all right here, *mon coeur?*"

Morgan smiled fondly. "I'll come with you. Maybe Del brought some sparkling cider."

The pair drifted deeper into the house, and Caleb turned to glance into the kitchen at the collection of family and friends, all eating, drinking, laughing, enjoying. Carlotta stood at the center of much of it, pouring beverages, handing out napkins, holding babies… God, she looked perfect in his world.

A loud honking outside signaled the arrival of the food. Caleb jogged outside, as did Tyler, Deke, and Logan, to help Luc and Alyssa in with the incredible smelling dishes that made him want to grab a fork and dig in now. Whatever Luc cooked, Caleb couldn't wait to eat.

It didn't take long before they had the banquet tables lined up in the great room with some folding chairs from the back of Luc's van. Del and Kimber had brought tablecloths and paper plates. Morgan produced plastic flatware from a bag in her purse. Tara rushed back to the car to fetch the table centerpiece while Alyssa set up the food station in the kitchen, her daughter Chloe hanging on her leg.

The gorgeous blonde bent to pick up her daughter and brush some tears from her face. "What's wrong, sweetie?"

Chloe pouted, her big blue eyes expressive. The girl would grow up to break hearts. "Boys."

Caleb laughed. Seth and Cal were forever fighting for Chloe's attention, but she sometimes got pushed or insulted when she wanted nothing to do with either of them.

"Here's a boy who will always treat you right." Alyssa turned to him with a smile. "Do you mind for a minute? I don't want her to burn herself."

Holding out his arms, he took Chloe from Alyssa's grasp so she could finish setting up the food.

The little minx threw her arms around his neck. "Hi, Unca Caleb."

"Hi, princess." He kissed her cheek. "What is Santa going to bring you?"

"Lots of toys. And no boys."

She'd changed her tune in a dozen years, but for now, he smiled and agreed.

The phone in his pocket vibrated, and Caleb shifted the little girl to one hip as he reached in to find the device and read the text from Hunter. "They're hitting the edge of town now," he told everyone. "They'll be here in less than twenty."

The party kicked into high gear then. Kimber rushed back to the car and produced a Christmas wreath for the front door. Deke followed with a nail, and they quickly hung it. Tyler and Logan trounced through the front yard, deciding at the last minute that it might be a good idea to string lights in the bushes. Delaney and Tara stood at the window watching them, shaking their heads.

"I've reproduced twice with that man," Del murmured. "I hope the gene pool survives."

Tara laughed. "I'm hoping we'll add to it soon, so we'll shallow it more. Then I'm sure I'll be second-guessing myself, too."

Del wished her good luck.

Out the big front window, Logan stopped to welcome someone who came up the walkway. Tyler greeted whoever it was as well. Caleb frowned. Were they expecting anyone else?

Finally, Logan opened the front door, and shouted, "More incoming." Then he turned behind him. "Glad you came."

His younger son bounded back outside to argue with Tyler about the lights, and Xander Santiago walked in the door. Caleb rushed forward. Chloe immediately started making starry eyes at the single billionaire playboy.

Xander, who'd walked in with a weary expression, laughed at Chloe. "That one is going to be dangerous."

Luc strutted past, carting two more platters of food. "Don't I know it! Anyone got a baseball bat? I'm suddenly feeling the need to start hitting teenage boys. Hey, Xander."

The other man sniffed. "Hi. Smells good, man."

"Thanks." With a nod, Luc continued to the kitchen.

"So how have you been?" Xander asked.

"Doing good. Great in fact." Caleb's gaze slipped over to Carlotta, and he felt his smile widening.

"Ah, so that's the way of things. Do Hunter and Kata know?"

"Yep, but even if they didn't, it wouldn't matter."

"Good for you." Xander smiled faintly.

He was a genuinely nice guy, usually a bit of a prankster. Today, he looked really damn somber.

"How is your brother?"

Xander shook his head, looking more than a little annoyed. "God, doesn't Logan keep anything to himself?"

Actually, Tyler had filled him in on the tragic murder of Xander's sister-in-law and the guilt spiral his brother, Javier, had been on ever since.

Caleb just shrugged, and Xander sighed heavily. "Thanks for asking. He's not doing well. He's trying to drink himself to death, and I had to have his stomach pumped about two weeks ago. He's alive and he's not terribly happy about it. I don't know what's going to make him want to live again."

"It will be something," Caleb assured. "I've seen guys come back from war and they're so traumatized..."

Of course not all of them pulled through, but if they had caring friends and families and the will to go on, they often not only functioned again but were damn happy. Even without saying it, Caleb saw that Xander loved his brother. Somehow, he'd pull his sibling out of the dark again.

"It will work out," he assured.

"I hope you're right."

Chloe wiggled out of his grasp and lunged at Xander, who chuckled and grabbed the little girl, mouthing a raspberry on her shoulder. The toddler giggled.

"You're a little flirt," Xander accused.

The little girl just batted her lashes.

As the men laughed, Caleb felt his phone vibrate again. He read Hunter's text with a wide grin.

"Two minutes, gang!" he shouted above the din of the party.

Instantly, everyone crowded into the kitchen, as Tyler and Jack killed the lights in the kitchen. Caleb did the same in the great room. Everyone lowered their voice to a whisper in anticipation of Hunter and Kata's big entrance. He sidled up behind Carlotta and slipped his hands around her waist, pressing a kiss to her neck.

"Hey, none of that now," Logan teased beside him.

Tara elbowed her husband.

Luc and Alyssa took advantage of the dark and shared a sweet kiss.

Jack pulled Morgan closer. In the shadows, it seemed baby Brice was asleep.

"Like hell," Jack groused. "This is the only time I get to touch my wife anymore. Don't mind us over in the corner," he told everyone.

Morgan giggled. "Stop that, Jack. Everyone will think I don't give you any attention."

"You know me. I can never get too much of you, *mon coeur*."

"TMI." Tyler shuddered.

A pair of headlights flashed through the front window. The car engine cut off. Two doors slammed.

"Where are we? Why are we here, Hunter?" Kata's voice sounded through the door as Hunter opened it for his wife and ushered her in.

Just then, the men flipped on the lights again and everyone

shouted, "Welcome home!"

Kata turned to her husband with a stunned looked, her mouth gaping open. "Home?"

Hunter caressed her cheek, then dropped his palm to her nape. "Yep. Our home, honey. I bought it for us. For the future. When my tour is up this summer, I'm going to take Jack and Deke up on their job offer. And we're going to have those babies."

She didn't say anything for a long moment, just stared at her husband. Then she screamed and threw herself into his arms. "Really? Seriously? You'd do that for me?"

"For us, honey. I want to be with you and I want to prove it."

Kata pressed a dozen kisses to his face, her arms hooked tightly around his neck. "I love you!"

"I love you, too." He held her tight and chuckled. "Do you want to see the rest of the house?"

"Absolutely!" Hunter led Kata off by the hand, and most of the crowd followed them for the nickel tour, slapping Hunter's back and congratulating the couple on their new place.

Their happiness warmed Caleb and gave him hope for his own future. When Carlotta started to follow her daughter and his son down the hall, he hooked an arm around her waist and held her back. "They don't need you right now, baby. I do."

Before she could question him, he claimed her lips in a slow kiss, taking her mouth gently and thoroughly until she melted against him. When she was putty under his hands, her lids fluttering open and her breathing heavy, he cupped her face and lifted her gaze to his.

"I love you, Carlotta."

She flushed sweetly, but didn't look away and didn't hesitate. "I love you too, Caleb."

Hope buoyed his heart...even if his guts felt as if they were running an obstacle course through slogging mud. He had been through a lot with this woman. A lot of worrying, a lot of waiting, a lot of uncertainty. But he was certain of this and their tomorrow.

Caleb fished into his pocket and withdrew a little black velvet box, then popped the lid open. "Marry me."

She gasped, her hands covering her mouth as her jaw dropped. Her big chocolate eyes widened. Then she dropped her hands and a huge grin curled up those red, sensual lips he was hungry to kiss again. "Really?"

"Really, Lottie. Be my wife."

"Yes!" Her happy shout echoed all through the house and brought everyone else running down the hall in a mass of whining toddlers, warriors on alert, and women eager for gossip. Caleb ignored them all as he grabbed the ring from the velvet case and slid it on Carlotta's finger.

The crowd all stopped short as tears slid down Carlotta's cheeks. In that moment, she had never looked more beautiful to him. She had never looked more his. And he could not remember ever feeling happier.

"Mamá?" Kata asked, almost as if holding her breath.

"You are not the only one in love with an Edgington man." Carlotta flushed.

Caleb laughed and picked her up with a whoop. Tara and Delaney dried their eyes. Kimber darted forward to hug her and welcome her into the family again. Logan pressed a kiss to her cheek. The rest smiled fondly, more than happy for another reason to celebrate. Except Xander, who looked like he might never be happy again. Caleb hoped for his sake that he could find even a fraction of the joy he felt now.

Elation bubbled inside him as he pressed Carlotta to him for a happy kiss.

"This is the best Christmas ever," she whispered to him.

"The very best," he agreed. "Let's get married by New Year's."

"What?" She looked startled. "Where? How? I don't have a dress."

"Vegas. Justice of the Peace. Caribbean island. I don't care where we are or what you wear. I don't want to wait another minute longer than I have to in order to hear you say 'I do.'"

"I'm stronger and happier for having you in my life, and I want to spend all my days loving you, Caleb. I do."

"I do, too. Now kiss me, baby."

To the whoops and catcalls of everyone around them, he claimed his fiancée's lips and held her tight, knowing this would be the first of many magical Christmases to come they would share.

Wicked To Love
A Wicked Lovers Novella

Shayla Black

Published by Shelley Bradley LLC

"What is the meaning of this?" Brandon Ross grabbed Emberlin Evans's arm before she could duck into her apartment.

As she gasped out a startled sound and turned to face him, Brandon fisted her letter between them. Goddamn it, he wanted an explanation for why she'd tossed this crap on his desk and left without a word.

Then he saw her face. Redness rimmed her swollen hazel eyes. Tears splashed down her mottled cheeks, rolling past her lips, which were pressed together in a grim line.

His anger evaporated, and he eased closer, relaxing his grip. "Em, are you all right?"

She pulled away, her pale hair like a cloud around her shoulders as she fumbled with her keys. "Fine. I've resigned, effective immediately. That's all you need to know."

What the hell? Legally, he wasn't entitled to know more, but personally? "Emmy, what happened? Did someone hurt you?"

"Not in the way you mean." She closed her eyes, refusing to look at him. "Just…go."

Fuck no. He'd seen Em cry once in the three years they'd worked together—the day she'd lost her mother. This wasn't the same calm assistant he'd relied on for everything from faultless organization to uncanny insight. Seeing her pain made his chest feel hollow and tight. Even if she wasn't going to work for him anymore, he refused to leave her upset.

"Tell me what's wrong, Em. Do you need help?"

"No." She edged behind the door, putting it between them, and set her keys on the counter. "I can't work for you anymore. My resignation letter says everything relevant."

"Except *why*."

Incredulity crossed her face. "Why do you care?"

"No one is more efficient or can more ruthlessly prep me for a meeting. You know this business. We've been a damn good team. I don't understand."

Em gripped the door between them. "You'll find someone else who's equally qualified."

"I don't want to find someone else. You're the best. Do you need more money? I'll do my damndest to get you a raise. You deserve it."

"It's not about money." She started to close the door, shutting him out.

Alarm set in, and Brandon wedged his foot inside, blocking her. He peeked through the crack. "Please. I...need you."

The thought of her not being his right hand stabbed him with panic. Nothing would run right without her. *He* wouldn't run right without her sassy finger wags, sparkling laughter, and ruthless organization.

But instead of coaxing, his admission seemed to crush her. Her face crumbled as more tears spilled. "No, you don't. You never will."

Brandon grabbed her shoulders and pulled her closer. Damn, she felt so fragile, so soft. "Why would you think that? We've worked hard to get the city to appropriate funds for the firefighters' new equipment. We won a major battle last Friday, and you were all smiles after that meeting. Without you, it's very possible their decision could have gone the other way."

"You'll manage just fine on your own. I need a...change. Could you please go?" Em shrugged away and tried to shut the door again.

"Bullshit." Brandon pushed it open wide and shoved inside. She was upset; no mistaking that. "I don't believe for one second that you're done helping Houston's first responders. You've worked your ass off for every victory. For three years you've talked about nothing except making sure other families don't lose a loved one in the line of duty, the way you lost your father. Championing his cause is your passion. I don't believe you want to give that up."

No fucking way would Brandon simply let Em go—not until he understood why she wanted to quit something so meaningful to her. Not until he did everything he could to help her.

She sniffled angrily. "You have no idea what I want."

Brandon still wasn't buying it, but he'd play along. "If you truly need a different job, I'll do my best to help you. As a boss, I'm really disappointed to lose you. But as your friend, I'm not leaving until—"

"Your friend?" She stared at the ceiling for a painful moment. When she looked at him, fresh tears glistened.

Oh, damn. She wasn't simply upset; she was upset with him. Was she quitting because of something he'd said or done?

"Emmy, tell me what I did to make you cry," he murmured. "Whatever it was, I didn't do it intentionally. I assumed we were friends, but if you don't want to be—"

Brandon clammed up, refusing to finish that sentence. It bugged him that she wouldn't think they were at least friends. No, the thought actually hurt.

Of course Em had worked for him, but they'd shared more than a job—at least he'd thought so. Brandon had held her hand at her mother's funeral. She'd nursed him back from that terrible flu last fall. She'd prepared a delicious Thanksgiving dinner for his half-sister Morgan and her husband, Jack, keeping the conversation rolling so that there'd been no awkward moments—a big plus since Brandon had once taken Jack's former wife to bed.

The same woman who had abruptly visited his office last Friday afternoon.

Shit. Did this have something to do with Kayla? Was Em...jealous? Brandon didn't hate that idea. No denying that Em was lovely. Her sweet face and blazing head for business were attraction enough. But she also had lush tits and a gorgeous ass with a tiny waist in between. How could he not notice her?

During their introduction, he'd put her in the "doable" category. Then the HR rep had informed him that Em was his secretary. After that, Brandon had done his best to put all sexual thoughts of her on lockdown and be strictly her boss. After all, Houstonians had elected him to do a job, not chase a skirt. The first few weeks of ignoring Emmy as a woman had been tough. Since then, they'd been so busy, and she'd been thoroughly professional. Once he'd gotten used to her as a co-worker, he'd stopped thinking about her as a woman.

Until now.

"I don't want to be friends, Brandon." Em braced her hands against his chest and gave him a little push. "Go, please."

Her touch flared sparks through him. Arousal charged his veins, seared his skin. Blood gushed south in a torrent. His dick got hard and strained against his zipper in record time.

Suddenly, he was rethinking the whole "friends" thing, too.

"I'm not leaving." Brandon kicked the door closed behind him, nudging her farther into her snug but homey apartment, backing her against the foyer wall.

He'd be damned if he simply gave up on her without a good reason.

Then her musky-floral scent teased his nose. Fuck, she even smelled good. His dick swelled more.

Eyes wide, she thrust her hands on the flare of her hips. "Well, come on in."

He ignored her sarcasm. "Why don't you want to be friends?"

At his question, she tried to edge away from him. No fucking way. Brandon planted his hands on the wall on either side of her head, caging her in, and leaned closer.

Em sighed in frustration. "Ease up. I need a tissue."

He reached over her and grabbed the little box off the bar, not giving her an inch of breathing room. He probably should, at least while she dabbed her face. But he wasn't letting her go until he had the answer to his question.

"Does your resignation have anything to do with Kayla's visit?"

Em got that deer-in-the-headlights look and drew in a sharp breath. *Bingo!* Why would Kayla's visit matter? It shouldn't…unless Em had feelings for him. Unless she wanted him. It took him barely half a second to realize that he really didn't hate that idea, either.

"Go, Brandon. Please."

They had to talk about this. Even if Em left her job, he didn't want matters unresolved between them. He wouldn't leave her hurting. But Em had been tight-lipped so far about answering his questions. If she had feelings for him, she wasn't going to blurt them. But he could test his theory. All it would take was one small kiss.

Brandon lowered his head. Her breath caught just as he layered his mouth across hers.

At the first touch of her pillowy lips, a jolt of heat blistered through him. He lingered, then pressed harder. She accepted his kiss, clung to him, her lips so pliant and eager. Em felt so damn good. Desire blindsided him. Unable to stop, Brandon went back for seconds, brushing his mouth over her softness again.

As he drew in a shuddering breath, her scent lured him closer. In fact, now that he was opening his senses to her, everything about Em intrigued him.

He wrapped his hands around the golden knot of hair at her nape and brought her even closer. Em's soft curves melted against him. The feel of her heart pounding furiously against his chest drugged his system with desire. She trembled in his arms as he laid yet another kiss on her little rosy mouth, then licked his way across her lower lip. He'd already taken more from her than a boss should, but now he knew that Em felt something beyond the professional for him.

When she mewled, that desperate little sound rolled through his blood like a fever. Arousal seized his spine and shook him to the core. Holy hell, Em was a fabulous assistant, but right now, he wanted her as a woman—naked, gasping, nails in his shoulders, crying his name.

Impatient and hungry, Brandon pushed his way inside her mouth and invaded deep to finally taste her. *Ah, so fucking sweet.* Sugary and a bit tart. Addicting.

She unfurled for him, tentatively at first. Then he brushed her tongue with his and took complete possession of her mouth. Em went wild, wrapping her arms around his neck, pressing her body so close not even a breath of air came between them.

Hot. Her sweet mouth beneath his welcomed, beckoned. And the little noises she made at the back of her throat... Then—*shit*— she wriggled her hips, rubbing her pussy against his iron-hard cock, conveying her need. A new spike of desire pierced him. His self-control gave way.

He grabbed her ass through her skirt, wedging her tightly between his body and the wall, thrusting right between her legs in an insistent rhythm that had her digging her nails into him and gasping out his name. *Fuck.* When was the last time he'd been this hot? This hard? She'd stunned him with her softness, her ardor. He needed more of her now.

When Brandon wedged a hand between them to cup her breast, he started to sweat. He'd suspected that Em had one hell of a rack under those boxy, professional jackets she wore, but even he'd been unprepared for how lush and real her curves were, how wonderfully heavy and firm her breast would lay in his palm.

Oh, God. This was his practical, efficient Em? She was like a world of secrets he'd never imagined and now couldn't wait to explore.

Somehow he managed to tear his lips away from hers. Her skin—he had to taste it. He brushed his lips over the pale flesh of her throat, latching on for a gentle nip, a lick. He groaned, savoring her. Her scent was something light, with a hint of cloves and spice. The texture of her skin was so silken it was almost powdery. Definitely delicate and pure. She burned easily in the sun. He'd heard her talk about it before and had laughed at her fragility. He'd usually dated outdoorsy girls. But now? They'd probably feel like leather. Em was a delectable, velvety treat. And if her neck was this soft, he could only imagine what he'd find between her breasts, across her stomach, on the insides of her thighs.

The thought made him harder than he could ever remember being in his life.

"Brandon," she breathed, clutching him tighter.

"Em, baby. God, you feel so good. You taste..." He captured her mouth again. He had no words to describe how unique and perfect her flavor was to him.

She welcomed every touch he gave her and shoved his suit coat off his shoulders, down his arms. Hugo Boss puddled at his feet behind him, and considering what he'd paid for this suit, he should care. He didn't. If her ripping out the zipper of these slacks would get him inside her faster, he was totally in favor.

He yanked her coat off, then went for the pins holding her golden tresses up at her nape. He tugged gently, sliding clips out. The strands fell apart to reveal soft waves that he wrapped in his fingers, anchoring her against him, just as he would when he got deep inside her and pumped her to orgasm.

Jesus, she hadn't said yes. She might push him away. If she did, he'd seduce, caress, beg—whatever it took. He craved her under him right now, taking him. He felt desperate to fill her with his cock.

Except...she'd left him today without a single word.

Too often, he dated damsels in distress, like he unconsciously sought someone to rescue. He and his half-sister Morgan had talked about the fact that he needed to stop chasing people who were fucked up. They always used him for cheap therapy, then tore his heart out when they left. Like Kayla. But if Em said yes now, it would be because she wanted *him*, not because she needed rescuing. She was one of the most grounded, genuine people he knew.

Em couldn't leave him now. *No way. Not happening.* He'd tasted her—and he was nowhere near done.

Finally, he peeled her jacket away and tossed it over the bar beside her. He tore into the shapeless blue blouse beneath her gray coat. He half-feared some resistance, but no. She pressed another kiss to his lips, then wrapped her fingers around the buttons of his shirt and unfastened them, one by one. He was all kinds of distracted by all the cleavage he exposed above that lacy, uber-sheer contraption she called a bra. Fuck, he could see her tight, pink nipples. And he could barely breathe.

When Em's small hands prowled across his bare chest, over every muscle and ridge, lighting up his skin more effectively than a hundred strings of Christmas lights on a tree, he lost patience and ripped the rest of her blouse away. Buttons popped off, flying everywhere. Silk shredded with an almost sexual roar that fired his blood hotter.

Em gasped as he dragged her shirt off and clasped her breasts in his palms. "Fuck, these are pretty. Em... God, I want these. I want you."

He couldn't wait to have her bra off. It clasped in the back, and he pulled at it with one hand while he nipped and sucked at her through the sheer cups.

Em gripped his hair, clasping him against her, and groaned a soft "yes."

One little word, and he became a freight train without brakes. She wanted him, and nothing was going to stop him from having her. In that moment, Brandon was damn glad, especially when the clasp of her bra gave way beneath his fingers and the little garment fell to the floor...

#

She was disintegrating. That's all Em could think as she opened beneath the dominating power of Brandon's kiss. He tasted like everything she'd imagined he would. Clean, strong, masculine, powerful. He didn't just part her lips with his; he plowed past her defenses and melted her resistance, her inhibition, her thoughts.

Sighing into his mouth, Em gave herself over to him completely.

She'd been in love with Brandon Ross from almost day one. When they'd first met, she'd seen a flare of attraction in his blue eyes. God, he'd only had to look at her, and she'd blushed thinking about all the heady, sexual things she wanted to do with him. But he'd quickly replaced that flicker of awareness with a professional mask. Together, they'd done a lot of good for the city's first responders, and she was proud of that. They'd also gotten to know one another. With every conversation and revelation, she'd only fallen deeper for her loyal but very sexy boss.

Then, a few months later, the Emergency Services taskforce team members had gone for happy hour following some victories with the city budget planners. Everyone had imbibed a drink or two, then left. She'd been alone with Brandon. After a few beers, he'd told her that he'd been in love with a former buddy's ex-wife for a few years.

Brandon's lack of interest in any other woman had made sense then. And it had broken Em's heart. But she'd lived with it, hoping that someday...

But someday had never come. Instead, after three years, his flame, Kayla, came to see him last Friday afternoon. When they'd left together in deep conversation, standing intimately close and looking beautiful together, it had crushed the last of Em's hope.

But now, Brandon wasn't kissing her like a man in love with someone else. His tongue curled around hers, tangling hotly. His hands clasped her face, holding her still so he could dive even deeper. He pressed his bare chest to hers like he wanted to meld into one body, like he found any separation between them unacceptable. Em couldn't agree more.

If she had any chance to have even a few hours with Brandon, she'd take it with both hands. It probably sounded pathetic, but she was past caring. This man had been the center of her fantasies and dreams for three years. She wasn't giving him up until he walked away.

Brandon ripped his mouth from her and stared down into her eyes. His wide, muscled chest rose and fell with every breath, but the electric connection of their gazes never wavered. Silently, he was asking what the hell was happening between them. She didn't want him to question, just kiss her again, take off the rest of her clothes, and make her his—even if it was only for a moment.

"Please..." she begged.

His eyes darkened. "I've got to have you, Em. Baby..."

She gave him a jerky nod, then stood on her tiptoes to kiss him.

He opened to her searching lips, then took control. The dark way he dominated her mouth made her shiver, especially when he thumbed her nipples, ripping fire through her. She gasped into his kiss and gripped his shoulders like she'd never let go.

With a last nip at her lower lip, he broke away and went straight for her breasts. He took her nipple into the hot cavern of his mouth and sucked hard. The sensation zipped a tingling path down to her pussy. Already, she could tell how wet she was. Her little panties were clinging damply to her flesh. And she ached so badly to have him filling her there.

His mouth found her other nipple. He pinched the first, still wet and stiff from his attention. With another moan, she cupped the back of his head. God, she could do this all day. The pulls of his mouth were so voracious, they were almost painful. Then he soothed her with tender little licks that made her melt into him even more.

Brandon tugged on the fastening of her skirt at the small of her back, but the complicated series of hooks weren't budging. He tried to rip it, the way he had her blouse. She could undo it herself, but it would take too long. She had to feel him now.

So Em pulled up the gray pencil skirt to her waist. Brandon didn't need more of an invitation. He shoved her little panties down her thighs. She wriggled until they hit the floor. But once the underwear was off, she had nothing to do but watch in rapt fascination as Brandon dropped to his knees and stared right at her pussy. He brushed his thumb over her slick folds, right over her clit. His tongue followed the same path.

She gasped. "Brandon!"

"Spread your legs, baby. I have to see you."

Whimpering, she complied. She had no idea what was running through his head as his hot breath feathered over her flesh. Em held her breath, wanting him so badly that she whimpered.

He fastened his mouth on her clit. Her entire body arched as a curl of arousal deepened into an aching need. She shoved her hands into his thick hair again, but nothing could anchor her against the dizzying pleasure as he sucked her clit deep.

"God, this sweet pussy…" he murmured against her flesh. "I didn't expect you to be bare. You're gorgeous. I want to stay here and feast."

If he did, she'd go mad. But if he left her, she'd go downright insane. "More."

"Oh, yeah. A lot more."

He buried his mouth between her legs again, parting her folds with his thumbs. This time he got closer, deeper, taking her completely in. He tongued her nub, and the friction made her body seize up. She pulled at his hair. Brandon didn't seem to mind. He merely caressed one thigh, then shoved it over his shoulder. The position left her wide open, and her other leg would have given out beneath her if he hadn't propped her against the wall.

God, with that kind of stimulation, Em couldn't hold still. She wriggled and whimpered, moaning his name, frantically trying to press closer to him. Again, Brandon took control and grabbed her hips.

"Em, hold still. Let me make you feel good."

She wanted that, but he was asking for the impossible. His unyielding grasp left her little choice. He forced her to take his tongue lashing. The coil of desire between her thighs tightened, ramping up until she could only pant and need and cry his name.

It had been so long since she'd felt a lover's touch. She hadn't wanted anyone but Brandon, and even her vibrator held little appeal these days. It couldn't make her feel beautiful. The hollow orgasms it delivered didn't make her feel desired or loved. Brandon did. Under his mouth, she felt like his most coveted treasure, and the way he ate at her like a delicate treat shoved her to the edge of pleasure.

"I'm going to come," she gasped out.

"Good. So sweet, Em. That's it. Come for me."

His next lick sent her flying into an ecstasy so white-hot, she could hardly comprehend it. Em screamed and bucked under his mouth. But Brandon didn't let up. He stayed with her through the giant rolling wave of sensation, his tongue flicking her pulsing nub, prolonging her pleasure, drawing it out until she was gasping and breathless and dizzy from the searing bliss.

She hadn't even caught her breath when Brandon straightened and pressed a voracious kiss against her lips. She tasted herself on his tongue. Em had never exchanged this intimacy with a lover, and Brandon seemed determined to share it with her. So she surrendered and welcomed him.

But she wanted more.

Thrusting her hands between them, she grabbed at the button of his slacks. He sucked in a breath as it came undone. The purr of his zipper lowering filled her ears, along with his moan. He shoved a hand into his pocket as she yanked his underwear to his hips, then dragged both garments to his ankles. A moment later, she heard the rip of foil and found him rolling a condom over his cock.

Em blinked as she watched. She'd thought he felt big as she'd rubbed against him. But seeing him? She wasn't terribly surprised that he was long. At something like six foot three, Brandon was tall, lean, and athletic. But the girth of his cock gave her pause. She'd read the clichés about penises that were supposedly several inches thick. She'd chalked it up to an urban legend or romantic drivel. She'd never seen a man packing that much in his Hanes.

Until now.

"Having second thoughts, Em?" he asked. His tight expression quietly suggested that if she said yes, it would kill him, but he'd accept it.

And honestly, she was—but not for the reason he imagined. Em hadn't slept with another man in over three years. She'd broken up with her last boyfriend six weeks before Brandon had joined their team. Since then, she'd done her best to satisfy herself with fantasies of her boss, with a little help from her battery-operated boyfriend.

But this flesh-and-blood man was much bigger.

"No." Her voice trembled. "I want this so bad."

That was the unvarnished truth. She'd never in her life ached for a man this way. Most she could take or leave. Even as a teenager, she'd never had a crush on a guy that she'd thought would kill her if her feelings went unreciprocated.

Brandon had changed that, too.

He swallowed. "Me, too. I didn't come here planning to even kiss you, much less get inside you. I…"

"I know, but I wouldn't change it. My bedroom is at the end of the hall."

He shook his head before she even finished speaking. "Too far away. I've got to fuck you now."

How did he plan—

Before she completed the thought, he bent and lifted her, shoving her back tight against the wall, holding her in place with the hot weight of his muscled body. She squealed and gripped his shoulders as he aligned himself with her swollen folds. *Standing up? Here? Now?*

His cock nudged her wet pussy. He quickly found her opening and tucked the head inside her. That touch filled her with electric need, as if she hadn't just had the monster orgasm of a lifetime minutes ago.

Then suddenly, he loosened his grip on her hips and let gravity do its work. She sank quickly onto the impaling breadth of his cock. Her breath hitched once, twice, again... God, he filled her so full, she thought she might burst. Her gaze flared wide, and Brandon watched her with a dark smile crossing his face.

"You feel me, baby?"

"Yes," she panted. How could she not? She stretched and burned. And even through the pain, it felt so good.

His smile turned a little warmer, then he kissed a path along her jaw. "You're so tight. You're like heaven."

He moaned and edged his hips away, withdrawing. Friction screamed along her sensitive nerve endings. Everything inside her ratcheted up again, and it was like she'd never come at all.

If she let him, Brandon would do all the work—and control the pace and depth of their lovemaking. But she wanted to get dirty with him, drown in him. She intended to enjoy this while it lasted.

Grabbing his face, she plastered her lips across his, then plunged into his mouth. He didn't resist a bit, merely opened wide to take her for a long, electric second. Then the jarring of his thrusts overtook everything. She wriggled on him, feeling her insides heat up, her breasts bounce, her pussy clamp down on him.

"You feel so fucking good," he growled against the curve of her breast. "How were you right in front of me for this long, and I didn't see you?"

Exactly what Em wanted to know, but she couldn't speak. Every drag of his cock inside her hit so many sensitive nerves that it made her nearly mindless. With each move, he stimulated her G-spot and bumped her cervix. She tightened, tightened, held her breath...

"Brandon..."

"You're going to come, baby, aren't you? I can feel you clenching that pussy on me. So responsive..." He pumped her harder, his fingers digging into her hips, and he moved under her in short, rhythmic strokes. "I'm not far behind you. Let go, and I'll catch you."

Em gave him a shaky nod and squirmed as he plowed into her again and again. He brushed her clit with every stroke. Still sensitive from her last orgasm, it didn't take much more to shove her to the precipice. And then she heard nothing but her heartbeat hammering in her ears, felt nothing but the pleasure crashing through her body like a maelstrom as he thrust deep, groaning long and low, the sound dripping with satisfaction.

His knees began to give way at the same time his arms did. Brandon pulled free of her body as she slid down the wall to her feet. The question of her own legs supporting her was touch and go, but she braced one elbow on the bar beside her and managed to stay upright. In front of her, Brandon put his hand on his hips and tried to catch his breath.

And it hit her. She'd just let her boss—former boss—fuck her in her foyer. Now what? Em hoped like hell he didn't regret it. That would hurt. She might later, but for different reasons. Right now, she was basking in the closeness they'd just shared and praying that he wouldn't throw on his clothes and run out as if his ass was on fire, then exit her life forever.

"What the hell happened?" He braced his hand on the wall above her, looking down into her eyes.

As she did anytime he got close, she lost herself in his searing, dark gaze. Her stomach tightened with nerves. Was it wrong to want him all over again, at least to be close to him for a while longer? If he didn't want to have sex with her again… well, she hadn't expected it in the first place. But a hug would be nice.

Needing contact, she reached up to touch his bare chest, as she had only minutes ago. But now that the passion was spent for the moment, she had no idea what he thought. If he was done with her. Everything felt awkward. Em lowered her hand.

She lifted her chin. "We got carried away. I won't say I'm sorry."

"Hell, I'm not sorry. Just stunned." He frowned, then took her hand, squeezing it. "Let's find the bedroom."

Did he want to have sex again?

Tamping down her excitement at the idea, she guided him down the shadowed hall. When she glanced over her shoulder at him, his gaze met hers with a probing expression. He was going to want to talk, and she didn't know what to say. Didn't the puddle of clothes they'd left behind and the passion they'd spent say enough for now? Dear god, was he going to bring up Kayla?

When they reached her bedroom, he pulled back her sage green comforter and settled her between the ivory Egyptian cotton sheets. Normally, all that soft thread count comforted her, but she watched, tense, as he prowled into the adjoining bathroom.

A moment later, he emerged, condom gone. He lifted the sheet and settled in beside her, watching her intently. She'd known him long enough to guess that he wanted to hear what she was thinking. Em didn't know what to say.

"Obviously, we have a lot to talk about," he murmured. "Let's start at the top. You were quitting because of Kayla's visit?"

Em swallowed a ball of nerves. Wow, he got right to the point. At work, he was politically savvy and found really gentle ways to phrase delicate matters. Not so now. His directness was disconcerting, but if he was going to be straight with her, she might as well do the same. After all, three years of suppressing her feelings hadn't gotten her anywhere.

But one question kept circling in her head: If Brandon was with his former friend's ex-wife now, why was he in bed with his secretary?

"You've said for years that you're in love with her. When she came to the office last Friday, and you left early with her..." God, she couldn't look at him and give him the words to break her heart. She rolled to her back and stared at the ceiling, covering her breasts with the sheet. "I invented reasons to call you over the weekend. A few times. You never answered. I assumed you were...busy."

"With Kayla? No." He sighed. "Em, we just had a drink together. She came to apologize for the way things ended all those years ago. She's apparently in therapy and looking for ways to mend fences so she can forgive herself."

"The way things ended?"

"Jack Cole was my friend. We had an affair...while he was still married to her. I never told you that part. I'm not proud of it. We weren't together long before she left me, too. I thought she was the one that got away or whatever, and I'd been carrying a torch for her."

Brandon paused, and Em worked up the courage to look his way. He was staring again, this time with an expression she couldn't begin to decipher.

"But you're not?" she blurted before she could stop herself.

He rolled on his side and braced his head on his hand. With his free hand, he gripped her hip and urged her to roll closer and face him. "No. The hour I spent with her surprised me. I felt nothing except sorry for her. She's really screwed up her life since she left me. She got married again, got divorced again. She drank a little too much. She's finding her way out now. I told her that I was happy for her if she was getting her head screwed on straight. But I turned down her invitation to go out sometime."

As he spoke, it was like the fist that had been clutching her heart painfully released little by little. She realized that she'd been holding her breath and let go. "Oh."

"So now I've spilled. Your turn."

Em tried to wriggle away, but Brandon wasn't having any of it. Being emotionally vulnerable to a man who'd never treated her as anything more than an efficient assistant was a little like bungee jumping—a whole lot of terrifying. Some people found it fun. She hadn't. She didn't think this was going to be worth many laughs, either. But she wasn't chickening out.

"I've...had feelings for you for a while. It seemed less painful to leave than watch you be happy with someone else."

"Just feelings? You quit a job you love to avoid me. You had sex with me when you thought I was committed to someone else."

God, what did he want? "Okay, strong feelings."

Brandon looked like he wanted to press harder, but he didn't. "Why didn't you tell me sooner? At least give me a hint?"

Em bit her lip. How could she answer that without baring her soul?

"Don't try to phrase things in a way you think will be easier for me to hear," he demanded. "Just say it."

She sighed and shook her head. "I thought you were in love with someone else. I had to see you every day, work with you. If I told you or hit on you, and you rejected me, it would have been awkward. I didn't want personal stuff in the way of all the good we're doing for the first responders. Some of the equipment we've recently pushed the city to buy would have saved my dad's life." She teared up. "I mean, it's been seven years since he died. I've gotten on with my life; he would have wanted it that way." She sniffled. "But I'm still damn angry that penny pinching contributed to his death. All I've ever wanted to do was keep another family from losing their loved one."

In fact, she didn't really want to leave her job now, but she'd been certain that Kayla was back in Brandon's life... And she'd been unable to pine for him any longer and live with the pain.

But since he wasn't carrying a torch for Kayla, what now?

#

"I know," he reassured, caressing her shoulder. "You've done a lot of good for the firefighters. Your father would be proud."

Inside, his thoughts raced. Em had hidden her feelings for him for weeks? Months? Years? All because she'd believed he would have chosen Kayla over her.

Maybe...she'd been right—until a few days ago. Before, he hadn't been able to let go of Kayla. She'd been like a ghost haunting him. Many times, he'd questioned what he'd done wrong to drive her away. Seeing Kayla again had enabled him to understand that he'd done nothing wrong. She hadn't been capable of love or devotion five years ago. They'd been all wrong for one another.

But maybe if Em had spoken up sooner, he would have looked at her in a whole new light and decided to let go of the past. It didn't really matter now. All that mattered was that Em had opened his eyes today. In fact, he couldn't stop staring at her.

"Um, I hope you didn't feel rejected earlier, in your foyer." He peered at her, watching her reaction. "If you did, I wasn't doing something right."

She flushed. God, he adored that pretty, pale skin. "Um, no. That was amazing."

"Had you imagined us before, together?"

Her gaze slid away and a fresh stain crept up her cheeks, but she nodded. "More than a few times."

Em had an advantage over him there, but Brandon was guessing that he had more experience. And his mind was much dirtier. Still, he was curious.

"Give me some examples."

She shrugged. "On a rainy Sunday, I'd imagine that we might curl up together and watch a football game or a movie. Sometimes, when I'd cook alone, I'd imagine you in the kitchen with me, nursing a glass of wine, maybe chopping a vegetable or basting meat. And I'd think of you next to me in bed, holding me as we drifted off to sleep."

Something wistful crossed her delicate face, and Brandon paused. Em's fantasies weren't just sexual. They were domestic.

Why didn't the idea of being that cozy with Em make him panic? He was close to thirty. Maybe he was having some natural instinct to finally settle down. Or was he okay with the idea because he was comfortable with Em? Because he more than liked her?

As he sorted through the tangle of thoughts and emotions, she began trailing a teasing fingertip from his Adam's apple down his chest, down his abdomen, down to his cock. Before she'd even reached her destination, he'd gone ridiculously hard again. Desire raged like a flash fire through him, heating him from the inside out. Every cell in his body demanded that he get on top of her, get inside her again, and take her once more.

She didn't help his self-control when she wrapped her small hand around his cock and stroked so slowly, he shuddered and groaned.

"Jesus, are you trying to undo me?"

Em sent a sly glance up at him from beneath her dark lashes, those hazel eyes sparkling. Something in his chest tightened.

"Is it working?"

Fuck, yes. But since he didn't feel capable of speaking when her thumb dusted the head of his cock, he just nodded. God, how could she arouse him again so quickly?

"Sometimes, I'd lie in bed and touch myself and imagine your hands gliding over my skin. I'd touch myself and pretend it was you pinching my nipples, rubbing my clit."

Brandon rolled to his back, his head hitting the mattress. Her words alone made his blood pressure shoot up fifty points. Right now, he could imagine himself squeezing the rosy tips of her breasts and toying with that responsive little clit. Her soft, insistent stroking of his cock was the worst kind of tease.

"Would you touch yourself until you came, baby?" he ground out. Imagining her masturbating to thoughts of him aroused him even more.

"Yes," she breathed.

He jerked his gaze to her. She fucking glowed—with the satisfaction he'd already given her, with the need for more. He didn't remember her ever looking more beautiful. In fact, he didn't remember being this close to a more beautiful woman. Again, he was left to wonder how he'd overlooked her for three years. Was he fucking blind? Granted, Kayla had left his thoughts, and Em had lost the boxy gray suit and efficient braid. Now, she looked relaxed and sexy. But what made her gorgeous to him was more fundamental.

She looked so lovely to him because she made him happy.

He froze at the realization.

"And sometimes, I'd close my eyes, use my vibrator, and fantasize that you were giving me that pleasure."

Oh, hell. She was trying to kill him. "Was the reality like you'd imagined?"

She shook her head, and a kittenish smile tilted up her swollen lips. "It was way better."

He raised a brow in a silent request for details. She knew him too well not to recognize it.

"You're human and real. I know how wonderful you are, dedicated and honest. The fact that you seemed to want me finally made it perfect."

"But?" he prompted. "I heard one in there."

"Well, you're, um…large."

He'd fucked her like a wild man against the wall. Brandon winced as he took hold of her wrist and stilled her hand. They needed to talk about this before she stroked him past coherent conversation. "Did I hurt you?"

Because if he had, he was going to kick his own ass.

Em hesitated and hedged. "A little. It had just been a while for me, but I'm fine."

"How long is a while?" Brandon had a sneaking suspicion, and if he was right, he was definitely going to kick his own ass.

"I don't know exactly, um…"

Bullshit. Em never didn't know something. She didn't want to tell him for some reason, and he planned to get to the bottom of it. "More than six months?"

"Yes."

"More than a year?"

She paused again, then sighed. "Yes."

He sat up and wrapped his arm around her waist, dragging her closer. "How much more than a year? Ballpark."

Those lush lashes of hers swept up, showing the alarm in her pretty green-gold eyes. Then she lowered them, the inky lashes brushing a milky cheek. God, she was so pretty and small. He'd given her no time to prepare for his cock to invade her body…

"Emmy?" he warned her.

Stiffening, she bit her lip. "A couple of months before you

joined the team."

"Over three years!"

She recoiled, and he grabbed her close, his palm sliding up and down her back in a soothing rhythm. Damn, he hadn't meant to scare her, *but three years?*

"Baby, I'm so sorry if I hurt you. I'll be gentle..." Next time? Would there be a next time? They still hadn't talked about her resignation. At the moment, he wasn't inclined to accept it. And if she came back to work, should he even be thinking about the next time he fucked her?

Too late. He was already thinking it.

Normally, he didn't believe in mixing business with pleasure. It was the primary reason he'd turned off his attraction to Em when they'd first been introduced. But now... He was pretty sure it was too late to put that cat back in the bag. He'd always admired her. But what he felt for Em after this morning had nothing to do with liking the way she kept a filing cabinet or drafted a meeting agenda.

"I know you will," she whispered, then slanted a sly grin his way. "Feel like proving it?"

His cock jerked, and he wanted so badly to shove his way between her pretty thighs and thrust deep inside of her again. But he had two problems.

"I don't have another condom."

Her smile widened, then she rolled over and reached into her nightstand drawer. She tossed it in his lap. A fresh box of ribbed condoms.

"I-I bought them after I invited you to dinner for your birthday last month. Just in case I worked up the nerve to proposition you, and you said yes."

Instead, he'd been called out of town on business at the last minute and canceled. Brandon was both staggered and completely flattered that she'd had seduction on her mind.

"Next problem?" Her grin came complete with a dimple, and she looked so adorably sexy. Something about her made him want to scoop her up, tickle her until she squealed and laughed, then fuck her senseless.

"You're going to be sore, baby. Even if I'm gentle with you..." He shook his head.

Suddenly, she grabbed the box and stashed it away. "It's fine. If you're not interested, I understand."

Brandon frowned. Em had jumped to conclusions, and after three years of his cluelessness, he could understand why. But when she stood and groped for her nearby bathrobe, he'd had enough. The idea that she was covering all her glorious pale skin, that he couldn't feel her naked against him, was not acceptable. They were going to get a few things straight right now.

Before Em could belt the robe, he grabbed it and pulled it off her body. She gasped and whirled on him. "Who said I wasn't interested?" He glanced down at his erection. "Do I look like I'm not interested?"

She glanced between his face and his cock. "So you're capable of an erection. That doesn't mean you're actually interested in me."

"Baby, there's no one else in the room. Trust me, I want you." He raised up on his knees and pulled her back to the bed. Her body was starchy and resistant at first, but a kiss and a palm cupping her breast fixed that.

"I really don't want to hurt you."

"If that was your only reservation, why wouldn't you let me tell you when I can't take anymore?" she challenged.

Brandon couldn't fault her logic. "All right. If you promise to tell me when you're too sore, I promise not to bring it up again. I'm sorry if you took my hesitation to mean that I didn't want you, Em. But you've spent some time thinking about us. I'm a little behind the curve. I'm so used to seeing you as professional and capable, not mind-blowingly sexy. Give me a little time to adjust. I'll get there."

And suddenly, he knew that he would. Fast. Already, he knew the idea of returning to their old relationship of strictly boss and employee wouldn't fly. The thought left a wretched taste in his mouth. But he also wanted her back professionally. So they were going to learn to navigate an office romance.

"Promise me that you'll only be with me if you truly want to," she demanded, but a hint of tears swam in her eyes.

Brandon had never seen Emmy vulnerable. It brought out all his protective instincts. God, he'd been such a blind idiot for the past three years. But he couldn't change the past now. All he could do was show her how much he wanted her, how rapidly she was becoming important to him.

"I want to be here, baby. Don't doubt that." He leaned closer and fused their mouths together. And he moaned. Somehow, she tasted even sweeter now. How was that possible? She'd already been addicting. Now, he absolutely craved her.

"Good. Can I..." She bit her lip again, and Brandon wanted to kiss it and make it all better. "Can I do something to you that I've been dying to?"

"I'm all yours." He rolled to his back and spread his arms wide.

She rose on her knees above him, her long, golden hair draping over her shoulders, brushing the slopes of her breasts and her nipples. Fuck, that was hot. But the vision of Em didn't just tug on his cock. Her tentative but curious expression hit him further north, square in the chest.

A moment later, she braced her hands on his shoulders, then ran her palms down his chest. She scraped her nails across his nipples, and he hissed. He was sensitive there, always had been. But her touch did something extra to him. When she followed the touch by dragging her hot little tongue across his nipple, Brandon thought he might come out of his skin.

Em nipped and sucked, tweaked and flicked. He closed his eyes. Arousal grew, climbed, until it clawed through his system. He groaned, bucked, his cock so hard now, it raged for her attention.

Brandon had engaged in nothing but casual sex for years. But nothing he was having with Em felt casual in the least. A need to take her, possess her, raged inside him. He was seconds away from turning caveman, from shoving her on her back and pumping her full of his cock until they both came.

Then Em clasped his erection again in her deft little hands. She bent, and her mouth followed. His world tilted. *Oh god.* He was going to die. The wet, hot silk of her mouth was going to kill him for sure. But he'd do it with a smile on his face.

Brandon groped around for something to fist. He couldn't find the blankets. He settled for Em's golden hair—and he used it ruthlessly, controlling the pace of her mouth over his throbbing dick. He pushed her faster, deeper, listening for any sounds of distress. She only moaned. Raising his hips, he fucked her mouth wildly. Such a tight fit. And she wasn't panicked or struggling. Em moaned and tried to take more, relaxing her throat. When she swallowed around the head of his cock, his eyes damn near rolled into the back of his head.

"Take me, Em," he growled. "Fuck, baby, that feels so good."

The way she panted around him, the flare of her tongue running up the underside of his dick, the long moments she spent laving that one sensitive spot just under the head, the grip she used to hold the inches she couldn't fit into her mouth, her little whimpers as she caressed his balls with tender fingers—they all stacked up, threatening to break down his control.

She'd keep going if he let her. She'd suck him to orgasm and swallow him down and expect nothing in return. Em was used to giving him what he wanted in a professional capacity. Over the years, he'd seen her support and help others, rarely having her kindness reciprocated. By not seeing her feelings and needs, he'd already hurt her over the last three years. Brandon refused to hurt her again now, especially when she felt uncertain and fragile.

"Em." He gently tugged on her hair to lift her heavenly mouth from his cock. Another day, he'd definitely want more of this. The thought of her sucking him off at his desk lashed arousal through his gut. It was unprofessional...but sexy as hell. Now just wasn't the time.

"Is something wrong?"

When he looked at her swollen pink mouth and dilated eyes, it was all Brandon could do to maintain his self-control. He drew in a ragged breath.

"No, baby. Come here." He opened his arms and pulled her closer, gratified when she snuggled her naked body against his. "Your mouth felt so good, but I want today to be about you."

"Why can't it be about us?"

The question seemed so simple, but those pretty hazel eyes of hers looked unsure. God, how could he erase her doubts and prove to her that he was serious?

Serious? Hell, he had no idea where this was going. An hour ago, she'd simply been his secretary. When he'd first touched her, he hadn't thought of anything beyond getting inside her. Then minutes ago, he'd been pondering an office fling. Now...implications of later were crashing in on him. She wasn't a fuck. As hungry as he felt for her now, it could be weeks, maybe months, before he'd had enough. But when he looked at Emmy, all disheveled and flushed, he wondered if he'd ever be able to get enough of her.

"You're right." He cupped her cheek. "Today should be about

us."

It should be about filling her up with as much desire as she'd given him. About…bonding. He'd never imagined that he'd want to do that with anyone except Kayla, but not having the woman weighing him down any longer was freeing. He could move on, fall for someone else.

When Em smiled up at him, Brandon couldn't resist her. He covered her lips with his, then sank into the heavenly warmth of her mouth. Em was so soft everywhere and had breasts straight from heaven, heavy and firm with wide pink nipples. Her hips filled his hands. She'd gloved his cock so tightly, and the sex had been amazing. But his desire for her wasn't really about that, at least not totally. He plain liked her and admired her wit, ambition, and loyalty. Her goodness had always pushed him to do and be better.

"I lost you somewhere," Em whispered. "Look, if you'd rather not do this—"

"That's not it. I realized this weekend that I'd wanted Kayla because she was stunningly beautiful and totally forbidden. The reality was, she was prone to drama, wanted to blame others for her problems without acknowledging how her own choices played a role, and she enjoyed being cared for more than she cared for anyone in return."

"Still, you cared about her." Em shrugged, but Brandon could see that it hurt her to say those words.

"I wanted to help her, and she was a beautiful woman, but I think I couldn't let her go mentally because, for me, she was all tangled up in disappointment and guilt. I fucked up a deep friendship with Jack Cole to be with Kayla, and in the end, she ran off without a word. I was angry. She left me to take care of everything, pick up all the pieces. I assumed that to hurt so much, I had to be in love."

"It makes sense," Em said supportively. But she was pulling away.

Brandon grabbed tight. "But I see now that I didn't respect her. So I could never be in love with her—ever. But I respect the hell out of you. I always have."

Em tried to suppress it, but her hopeful smile did something to Brandon's heart. It flipped in his chest as he reached into her nightstand and grabbed the box of condoms. He tore it open and grabbed a few out, placing them on the nightstand.

Her eyes widened, and he grinned. "You say when, baby. Until then, I'm not letting you out of bed."

A kittenish smile crossed her face. "Promise?"

"You don't know what kind of day you're in for, but you're about to find out," he growled. "Roll over."

Without hesitation, she complied, and her complete trust in him did something to his libido. Though revved up and hot to get deep inside Em again, he forced himself to slow down. He had to make sure she was ready. The sex in the foyer had barely taken the edge off his hunger, and he wasn't sure how easy he could go on her once he felt her silken walls surrounding him.

Palming one of the condoms, he lay over her back, supporting most of his weight on his elbows. He swept his lips over her neck, dusting hot breaths and kisses across her sensitive skin, nipping and laving, loving every gasp and shudder he wrung out of her.

"You're going to feel so good, baby. I can't wait to fuck you again."

"Now." Her voice trembled.

"Soon."

He slid his hands under her body, palming her breasts, toying with her nipples. Under him, her body stiffened, and she arched into his touch. Plucking, scraping, twisting her nipples, he worked his mouth down to her shoulder.

"Your skin is flushing. You look so pretty. Are you wet for me?"

She nodded, moaned.

"You sure? Tell me," he demanded.

"Yes. Stop playing games."

"And fuck you?"

"Now." She fisted the sheets underneath her.

Just to be certain she could accommodate him with minimal pain, Brandon wedged a hand under her hip, to her pussy. He found the damp spot on the sheet before he touched her drenched folds. She was more than ready.

"On your hands and knees," he ordered.

As she complied, he leaned around her body and reached in the nightstand drawer for one more thing he'd seen earlier. Grabbing the little yellow contraption, he shoved it between his knees, out of her line of sight, then gripped Em's hips.

"God, you're beautiful, baby. So small and delicate, but here…" He caressed her ass. "And those breasts of yours…so lush."

"Brandon, you're killing me. Please."

Her whimper of need only made him harder. After quickly sheathing himself, he aligned his cock and began the slow slide into heaven. Her pussy clung to him, gripping so tightly, clutching when he withdrew even a fraction. *Damn.* Her little pants and mewls drove him even more insane.

He braced one hand near hers, and she covered it with her own, curling their fingers together. For some reason, that got to him. Everything about her made him want more. He could do this to her all day, all night, and still ache to fuck her tomorrow. Hell, he was happy just being near her. When had he ever felt *that* with any woman?

His balls tightened. So did his chest. He wrapped his arm around her middle and tried to unravel her one slow thrust at a time. But these leisurely glides were killing him, too. He buried his face in her neck. She smelled like spice, like female and sex.

Em moaned his name. "Faster. Harder!"

He wanted to draw this out, fire her up slowly. But with Em, the tight leash he normally kept on himself wasn't working.

"Hold on, baby."

Brandon reached for the little plastic unit he'd placed between his knees. With one hand, he turned it on. With the other, he placed the little vibrating rabbit right against her clit. As she gasped in pleasure, he slammed back inside her cunt, all the way to the hilt. Then he set a relentless rhythm, every thrust of his body demanding she come for him.

She tightened, trembled—her legs, her back, her pussy. He slid the little vibrating toy over her clit again, ruthlessly flicking it over the most sensitive part of her little bud until she clawed the sheets, heaved in a huge breath, keened in a high, tight cry.

"That's it. Come for me, Emmy. Let me feel you."

The fluttering walls of her sex clamped down on him, sucking him deeper, making it damn near impossible to move. Fuck, that felt good. And when she all but growled out her release, it somehow aroused him even more. It was hot. *She* was hot. But he wasn't ready to give into the pleasure searing his spine yet.

Brandon tossed the toy on the nightstand, withdrew from her

body, and flipped her to her back. Em barely had time to blink up at him before he shoved her legs wide, climbed between them, and slid deep.

With his cock nudging her cervix, he arched to penetrate her even more. Her nails clawed at his back as she tilted up to meet him, taking him deeper still. But it wasn't enough. He had to be the man who'd given her the most pleasure ever, the one she wanted above all others. The person she turned to when she laughed or cried, railed or teased. He definitely wanted to be the man she thought of when she came. He vowed to do whatever it took to be that man for her.

Unleashing every bit of his need, he fucked her with long, deliberate strokes, hitting her sensitive spots, circling his hips to hit them again and again, even as his thumb toyed with her clit. He didn't pause, didn't let up until she screamed out again, this orgasm so powerful, it threw him over the edge into an apocalypse of pleasure unlike anything he'd ever felt. He shouted her name, the edges of his vision going black as he released everything he had inside her.

Long minutes later, he withdrew from her limp, sated body, disposed of the condom, and curled up around her. Almost immediately, the need to be with her, inside her again, hit him. It wasn't purely sexual, though he loved making love to her. He wanted to…connect with her on a level that was deeper still. Cement their bond. Brandon frowned. He'd always liked Em, respected the hell out of her. But this feeling was totally new. Exactly how deep did his feelings run?

Before he could follow that train of thought, he heard the chirping of his cell phone from the front of her apartment. And he remembered it was Monday morning. He hadn't told a soul where he was going, simply ran out of the office, followed Em through the parking lot, and peeled out before following her here.

"Please tell me it's not eleven o'clock," he muttered.

Em glanced at the clock. "It's eleven fifteen. And that ring tone is the mayor's."

She'd know. She'd set it.

Grimacing, he jumped up and grabbed his cell just before the voicemail kicked in. "Hello, sir."

Brandon grimaced and listened to the testy politician, interjecting affirmative sounds when appropriate. Inside, he wanted to scream. Yes, this fucking meeting was important.

But so was Em, damn it.

Still, if he wanted to implement the sweeping changes that he and Em had worked so hard for, he had to leave now.

Quickly, he thrust on his clothes, then whirled for the bedroom. Instead, he found Em standing a few feet away in her big terrycloth bathrobe. "You're leaving."

"This is the meeting with the mayor and his staff. We have to talk about how to appropriate the new budget money, assess the needs of each fire station and allocate funds and equipment—"

"I know." She smiled sadly. "I set up the meeting for you. I left you prep notes on your desk Friday afternoon."

Of course she had.

"I don't want to leave you, Em. I'd rather stay with you all day."

"You have to go. Give those firefighters what they need to get the job done. Don't let anyone else lose a husband, father, brother, or son."

Brandon hated going now, but she was right. It had taken months to win the budget victory. If the mayor was willing to meet with all the players and get this done now, he couldn't throw that away. The opportunity wouldn't come around again soon, and he was already late.

He slanted a hard kiss over her mouth. "After this meeting, we're going to talk."

She nodded, handed him his keys from the bar, then opened the door. "Sure."

Nothing about her tone sounded happy, and he couldn't fix it now. He'd show her later.

"Seriously." He forced her gaze to meet his. "We will talk about this later."

Then Brandon left. Making record time to the office, he grabbed her notes and charged into the meeting, all apologies, then dug into the business at hand. A million times, his mind wandered to Em. Every time, he forced his thoughts back. He gave his full concentration so no other firefighter lost their life for so senseless a reason as poor planning. In the end, thanks in large part to her notes, he negotiated the best deal. Em would be both delighted and proud.

The second he left the meeting, he replayed their morning together over and over. They'd leapt from being boss and assistant, from being friends, straight into being lovers. No question, Em had started a fever inside him. A few hours away from her, and already he hungered to touch her again. But he didn't just crave the sex, hot though it was. He cared deeply about her happiness. He'd do damn near anything to reassure her that he was there with and for her. Caring, respect, friendship...weren't those good places to start building an actual relationship?

"Good meeting, Ross." The mayor shook his hand. As they walked to the elevator, he leaned in with a grin. "Whoever she is, since she's making you smile, I'm guessing she was worth the tardiness and distraction."

Brandon didn't even question how the mayor had known. After all, he'd shown up late with mussed hair and wrinkled clothes. But he'd gotten the job done, and now it was time to see Em. And to tell her the good news.

On his way to her place, he stopped for flowers and a bottle of her favorite wine. He also changed into jeans and a T-shirt. As he wandered down the hall of his house, he stared into all the half-empty bedrooms he'd originally intended to fill with a wife and children someday. After Kayla's departure, he hadn't let anyone into his life so he could make that happen.

Was Em that someone?

The question almost bowled him over. He'd had a handful of hours to think of her as a lover. Was he really already thinking about her as a wife? A mother? She loved with her whole heart, and he couldn't do better. He also wasn't sure he could do without her any more.

Taking a deep breath, he hopped back into his car and took a winding ribbon of side streets to beat the Houston traffic and reach Em sooner. When he parked his car, he damn near ran up the stairs, roses and wine in hand, and pounded on her door.

When she opened to him, Brandon found her in a simple tank top and capri pants that hugged the sweet curve of her hips. Instantly, he remembered the taste of her kiss, the way she looked at him like he was her everything as he filled her full of his cock, her crying out his name as she came. The adoration in her eyes when he cuddled her afterward. The gentle way she glowed as she smiled with happiness.

Damn, he'd been blind. Question was, what was he going to do about it?

"Hi, baby. We got everything we wanted for the firefighters."

"Really?" She smiled brightly and clapped her hands.

When she didn't throw herself into his arms, he stepped inside Em's place, grabbed her, and hugged her against him. "Really. It was perfect."

"Thank you. You fought a great fight."

"We did. How was your day?"

Tensing suddenly, she took the wine from him, then walked into the next room, setting the bottle in the refrigerator to chill. After that, she busied herself by finding a vase for the roses and adding water. "Fine. I've been thinking."

That sounded ominous. "Go ahead."

"You were right; I realized today that I can't turn my back on helping the firefighters. It's my passion. My dad wouldn't have wanted me to quit, and I won't give up. So if my job is still open, I'd like it back, starting tomorrow."

"Of course. Absolutely." In fact, that was a huge relief to him. He'd been willing to let her go if she didn't feel that she could work for him and be with him romantically, but if she could handle it, so could he. "I wouldn't want anyone else to be my right hand. The firefighters couldn't find a better advocate anywhere."

He groped around on the pass-through bar between her foyer and her kitchen until he found her resignation letter, the one that had given him the kick in the ass he needed to question everything. He ripped it in half, then crumpled it and tossed it into the nearby bin.

"There. Done." He beamed.

"Good," she said tightly, then she took a nervous breath, and Brandon's gut curdled up in alarm. "But I don't think we should sleep together anymore." When he opened his mouth, she cut him off. "I know you're not in love with Kayla. And I absolutely enjoyed being with you this morning. I've never had anyone who made me feel so good, who cared so much about my pleasure. With you, I felt sexy."

"You *are* sexy."

Em arranged the roses in the vase, then set them on the counter beside her. "Thank you. But I can't do 'just sex' with you. I know you've had a handful of hours to think about us together, but I have to be completely honest. I'm not built for casual sex. Nothing about you is casual for me."

"Emmy, baby—"

"Let me finish." She paced into the living room, putting the sofa between them. "I don't see any reason to give you less than the truth. I love you."

Those three words sent electricity skittering across his skin. He'd been hard when he'd knocked on her door. But now, he was like steel. He couldn't wait to touch her, get inside her, and show her how he felt.

"If you don't think you're ever going to be able to feel the same, let's not continue this, Brandon."

It had cost her a lot to say that, he could tell. And he understood where she was coming from. She'd wasted three years on a man too mired in the past to notice her. Now, she assumed a lot about his feelings—or lack thereof. "You're not casual for me, either, Em. I may have come late to the party, I may have been blind for most of our time together, but this morning, with one kiss, you opened my eyes. You know how much I rely on you at the office."

Em scoffed. "You'd be lost without me. You definitely can't keep a functioning calendar. Papers and e-mails would be everywhere. You'd rarely remember to return a phone call."

"Right. I'm a train wreck. But I'd give you up professionally before I'd give you up romantically. I really want you back in the office, but I'm pretty damn sure that I need you in my life and that I'm not going to be complete or happy until I'm sure you're mine."

A tremulous smile crept up her face. "Yours, huh?"

Brandon made his way around the sofa and took one of Em's hands in his. "Yeah. I'm pretty sure I'm falling in love with you, Em." He placed her hand over his heart, thrilled when she met his stare and he saw her love—her very soul—opening and shining from her eyes. "Stay with me, baby. Give me time to catch up and make you happy. If you want to be hands off until then, I totally understand. I want you to be comfortable. To trust me. I'll wait—"

"If that's how you feel, I don't want to wait." Her green-gold eyes danced with happiness—and a bit of mischief—as she stepped closer and pressed a kiss to his mouth. "I want you now."

He swallowed. His cock got harder. The idea of having Em every day by his side, every night in his bed, was beyond seductive. He wanted her every which way he could get her, whether that was naked against his sheets, just holding his hand, or giving him that secret grin at the office between meetings. He wanted every chance to fall completely in love with her and show her exactly how he felt.

But he wanted her ready and trusting. "Baby, I don't want to do anything until you're sure you're ready."

"Brandon." She cocked her head to the side.

"Yeah?"

Em brushed a palm down his chest, past his abdomen, farther south until she gripped his erection in her hand. "Take off your clothes."

Damn, her touch felt so good, Brandon thought he was going to swallow his tongue. But first things first. "Are you going to give me the chance to show you that I not only want you but care?"

"I can't wait," she breathed.

"Good. Then I've got an idea: Why don't *you* take *your* clothes off. Slowly. And let me kiss every inch along the way."

She grinned and reached for the little strap of her tank top. "Yes, boss."

Read on for excerpts from more exciting titles by Shayla Black and other talanted authors.

About the Author:

Shayla Black (aka Shelley Bradley) is the New York Times and USA Today bestselling author of over 30 sizzling contemporary, erotic, paranormal, and historical romances for multiple print, electronic, and audio publishers. She lives in Texas with her husband, munchkin, and one very spoiled cat. In her "free" time, she enjoys reality TV, reading and listening to an eclectic blend of music.

Shayla's work has been translated in about a dozen languages. She has also received or been nominated for The Passionate Plume, The Holt Medallion, Colorado Romance Writers Award of Excellence, and the National Reader's Choice Awards. RT Bookclub has twice nominated her for Best Erotic Romance of the year, as well as awarded her several Top Picks, and a KISS Hero Award.

A writing risk-taker, Shayla enjoys tackling writing challenges with every book.

Connect with me online:

Shayla Black:
Facebook: www.facebook.com/ShaylaBlackAuthor
Twitter: www.twitter.com/@shayla_black
Smashwords: www.smashwords.com/profile/view/ShaylaBlack
Website: www.shaylablack.com

Also from Shayla Black/Shelley Bradley:
EROTIC ROMANCE
THE WICKED LOVERS
Wicked Ties
Decadent
Delicious
Surrender To Me
Belong To Me
"Wicked to Love" (e-novella)
Mine To Hold
"Wicked All The Way" (e-novella)
Coming Soon:
Ours To Love
"Wicked All Night" - Wicked And Dangerous Anthology

SEXY CAPERS
Bound And Determined
Strip Search
"Arresting Desire" – Hot In Handcuffs Anthology

MASTERS OF MÉNAGE (by Shayla Black and Lexi Blake)
Their Virgin Captive
Their Virgin's Secret
Their Virgin Concubine
Coming Soon:
Their Virgin Princess
Their Virgin Hostage

DOMS OF HER LIFE (by Shayla Black, Jenna Jacob, and Isabella LaPearl)
One Dom To Love
Coming Soon:
The Young And The Submissive

Stand Alone Titles
Naughty Little Secret (as Shelley Bradley)
"Watch Me" – Sneak Peek Anthology (as Shelley Bradley)
Dangerous Boys And Their Toy
"Her Fantasy Men" – Four Play Anthology

116

PARANORMAL ROMANCE
THE DOOMSDAY BRETHREN
Tempt Me With Darkness
"Fated" (e-novella)
Seduce Me In Shadow
Possess Me At Midnight
"Mated" – Haunted By Your Touch Anthology
Entice Me At Twilight
Embrace Me At Dawn

HISTORICAL ROMANCE (as Shelley Bradley)
The Lady And The Dragon
One Wicked Night
Strictly Seduction
Strictly Forbidden
Coming Soon:
His Lady Bride, Brothers in Arms (Book 1)
His Stolen Bride, Brothers in Arms (Book 2)
His Rebel Bride, Brothers in Arms (Book 3)

CONTEMPORARY ROMANCE (as Shelley Bradley)
A Perfect Match

OURS TO LOVE
Wicked Lovers, book 7
Available May 7, 2013
By Shayla Black

Between two brothers...

Xander Santiago spent years living it up as a billionaire playboy. Never given a chance to lead his family business in the boardroom, he became a Master in the bedroom instead. His older brother inherited the company and worked tirelessly to make it an empire. But while the cutthroat corporate espionage took its toll on Javier, nothing was as devastating as the seemingly senseless murder of his wife. It propelled him into a year of punishing rage and guilt...until Xander came to his rescue.

Comes an irresistible woman ...

Eager to rejuvenate Javier's life, Xander shanghais him to Louisiana where they meet the beautiful London McLane. After surviving a decade of tragedy and struggle, London is determined to make a fresh start—and these sexy billionaire brothers are more than willing to help. In every way. And London is stunned to find herself open to every heated suggestion...and desperately hoping that her love will heal them.

And inescapable danger ...

But a killer with a hidden motive is watching, on a single-minded mission to destroy everything the Santiago brothers hold dear, especially London. And as fear and desire collide, every passionate beat of her heart could be her last.

EXCERPT

"I'm sorry if I startled you. Your dance was so sweetly seductive, I couldn't pass up the opportunity to express my appreciation. In fact, I'd like to appreciate you even more. What's your name, *belleza*?"

In case he was a rapist, she didn't feel the need to be polite. "You need to leave."

He held up both hands in a gesture meant to convey that he was harmless—not that she believed it. She scrambled back.

"Stop. Breathe. Listen." His voice dropped an octave as he stepped forward again.

Instantly, she found herself following instructions, then wondered why. Something in his voice maybe? It carried a stern note of a command, but his expression read gentle. Whatever it was, London responded. She dropped her gaze to the scratched-up stage, frantically trying to gather her thoughts.

"Good girl, *belleza*. I'm not going to hurt you. Relax."

Again, she found herself doing as he bid and being oddly happy that he'd praised her. Almost proud. God, was she so thirsty for something good in her life that she'd fall for kind words from a potential ax murderer?

"Nothing to worry about," he promised. "I'm a friend of Alyssa Traverson, the owner."

That raised her hackles. He should have stuck to the truth and said he was simply a customer. "I know most of her friends. I don't know you. What's your name?"

"I'm Xander."

The Xander? Logan's billionaire playboy pal? He was dressed expensively. Though Xander's eyes appeared hazel, rather than blue like his brother's, he looked enough like Javier otherwise—ungodly handsome—to convince her she'd guessed right.

The good news was, if he was a friend of Logan's, he wasn't an ax murderer or a rapist. In fact, she'd heard the stories about the ways in which Xander had helped both Logan and Tyler save their wives from some really dangerous situations. From everything she could tell, both of those men had great creep radars, so Xander wasn't a psycho.

But he was unnerving. She'd read about men who could make a woman's heart skip a bit, but London had believed it was all crap until recently. Xander and Javier were both lip-bitingly hot.

"What's your name?" Xander asked.

"L-London."

"Like the city?" he smiled.

She nodded. Hell, his gaze was so fixed on her that her brain shut down. When he looked at her like that, she couldn't think of anything to say.

"Have you ever been there?"

"No." She tried to smile. "Someday."

"You should see it." He smiled. "It's unique. And beautiful, just like you, *belleza*."

"What does that mean?"

"Beauty."

Exactly what his brother had murmured to her in his stupor.

"Don't frown at me. You looked gorgeous onstage. Do you dance here?"

Was he kidding? In the thong she was still wearing—with little else to cover her—she scrambled back to find her clothes, grabbing her blouse first and holding it up over her torso. She'd been so startled, then blinded by his gorgeousness, she'd forgotten that she was damn-near naked.

He laughed. "Hmm, covered or not, you're still sexy. You have the most tempting sugary pink nipples."

London spread her shirt across her breasts even as she felt heat crawl up her cheeks. "You can't see that. I'm wearing a bra."

"Made of peekaboo lace."

A quick glace down proved him right, and since her thong was made out of the same fabric, the chances were that he could see pretty much everything down there, too. Mortification swept over her in a hot wave. It shouldn't bother her, really. So many doctors and medical professionals over the years had seen her mostly naked, but those people had looked at her like a specimen. Xander stared at her like a predator sizing up a meal. Hungry. Intense. His gaze heated. Desire simmered. And she couldn't help but respond. Yes, she was flattered, but more, she felt an answering flutter between her legs.

"Could you . . ." She bit her lip, then forced her words out. "Could you be a gentleman and turn around so I can get dressed?"

He shrugged, but quirked a smile in her direction that said he'd be working to get her out of those clothes again soon. "Sure."

"Thank you," she said stiffly as he turned away.

She struggled into her clothes, tugging up her cargo capri pants, shrugging into her floral blouse with shaking fingers. This was the prudent thing, walking away from a womanizer already eyeing her. She had no experience with that kind of man—or any kind, for that matter.

But wasn't that why she'd left her mom's house and moved here, to break away from the shadow of her illness and go to a place where no one knew or remembered the tragedy of her adolescence? So she could finally experience life. So she could truly *live*.

Absolutely.

So Xander wasn't going to win any husband-of-the-year awards. London wasn't looking to get married. Sure, she'd like to have a boyfriend someday. Right now, all she wanted to do was meet people, date, and okay, maybe have a little sex. Or a lot. She had as much libido as the next girl, maybe more since she didn't exactly know what she was missing out on. But books and movies provided tantalizing glimpses. Even if it wasn't like all the glorified fictional accounts, well . . . then she'd know, right? She could finally say she'd experienced something—with a man who knew what the hell he was doing. If Xander had slept with that many women, why would he mind one more? She doubted that her virginity or her past would even matter to him.

Decision made, London loosened her top button and pulled aside the edges of her blouse so he'd get a good glimpse at her cleavage. "You can turn around now."

He did, appreciation lighting his eyes instantly. "Lovely. I didn't mean to scare you or peek uninvited. The door was open, I walked in, and you looked so beautiful that I simply couldn't stop you. So glad I didn't."

Xander reached out slowly, seeming to give her plenty of opportunity to back away. Heat rushed up her body. Her heart chugged and pulsed violently, but she refused to give in to the urge to scamper away.

With a reassuring smile, he helped her off the stage, then curled his fingers around her elbow with a proprietary grip, using it to draw her closer. "Come with me. Sit and talk." The words were half-request, half-command. He gestured to the club's dark bar. London didn't see the harm.

"All right."

"Excellent. I can't promise that I won't try to proposition you, but you're always free to say no." He sent her a disarming grin. "I'd like to get to know you. For now, I'll keep my hands to myself," he promised. "Mostly. Until you tell me otherwise."

London hesitated, trying to think things through, but it was damn difficult with him so near. "You don't give up, do you?"

"Not when I want something."

ONE DOM TO LOVE
The Doms Of Her Life, book 1
Available Now
By Shayla Black, Jenna Jacob, and Isabella LaPearl

Raine Kendall has been in love with her boss, Macen Hammerman, for years. Determined to make the man notice that she's a grown woman with desires and needs, she pours out her heart and offers her body to him—only to be crushingly rejected. But when his friend, very single, very sexy Liam O'Neill watches the other Dom refuse to act on his obvious feelings for Raine, he resolves to step in and do whatever it takes to help Hammer find happiness again, even rousing his friend's possessive instincts by making the girl a proposition too tempting to refuse. But he never imagines that he'll end up falling for her himself.

Hammer has buried his lust for Raine for years. After rescuing the budding runaway from an alley behind his exclusive BDSM Dungeon, he has come to covet the pretty submissive. But tragedy has taught him that he can never be what she needs. So he watches over her while struggling to keep his distance. Liam's crafty plan blindsides Hammer, especially when he sees how determined his friend is to possess Raine for his own. Hammer isn't ready to give the lovely submissive over to any other Dom, but can he heal from his past and fight for her? Or will he lose Raine if she truly gives herself—heart, body, and soul—to Liam?

EXCERPT

Liam raised his fist and knocked on the door. Raine whipped her head around, hope brimming in her eyes. It visibly died when she realized he wasn't Hammer.

She surprised him when she cast her gaze to the floor submissively. "Hi, Liam. Sir. Um, if you're here because you're worried or something, I'll be fine. I'll bake a batch of chocolate chip cookies and be as good as new."

So sweet. And lying. Eventually, he'd both soothe and paddle her until she learned to be honest, but for now he simply tried to set her at ease. "While I've little doubt about your culinary skills, since your baked goods are most excellent, I doubt they'll mend your woes, lass. Show me your hands."

Obediently, Raine held them out. Liam stepped closer, taking her wrists in his grip and examining her fingers. "You've a few wee cuts, but nothing serious." He gave her a smile and gently kissed her palm. "I think you'll live."

She stiffened. "I told you I'm fine."

"Your hands, yes. What about your heart?" He watched her shoulders slump. "I've come with a proposition. Would you hear me out?"

He had to win her consent—and give her hope—or she would leave and take Hammer's only chance of healing with her.

Raine sent him a wary glance. "I guess."

Liam sidled closer cautiously, careful not to give her cause to bolt. "Would you be adverse to me training you?"

At his words, her startling blue eyes widened, sucking him in like a whirlpool. He'd surprised her. Almost an instant later, she opened her mouth, regret already softening her face.

Before she could refuse him, he cut in. "How much longer will you let your own happiness be denied? Why not seek it with someone ready to appreciate the beauty you are?"

He watched her, following her every nervous gesture: her slight shrug, the tilt of her head, the rise and fall of her chest, the cant of her hip as she leaned back against the counter. Her innate grace and the subtle feminine scent he inhaled as he drew closer sent blood rushing to his cock unexpectedly. The primal reaction surprised him, but he was male, and Raine was lovely, after all.

As he looked into her haunting eyes, he knew yet another reason Hammer had kept this one for his own. Innocence. Fear. Hunger. A swirling mirror to her soul lay just beyond reach. Interesting. A heady challenge.

She bit the fullness of her lower lip. It only took that instant to make him want to comfort her. But that wasn't all. Lust to taste her sweet mouth, touch her, lay her back and—

He shoved the urge down and told his stiff cock to take a rest.

"I don't understand." She blinked up at him. "You want to train…me?"

"I think you need it. And you deserve it. I admire your spirit and your grace. I can't imagine that you want to wilt away, pining for unrequited love."

Her mouth pinched. "What's in it for you? You saw my stupid display earlier."

The girl needed reassurance. Liam reached for her and pulled her into his arms. The act nestled her pillowy breasts against his chest, her soft curves against his body. An intriguing musky lily scent wafted from her pale, smooth skin. A vision flashed across his brain of Raine beneath him, crying out as he fucked his way deep inside her.

Liam sucked in a shocked breath. He forced himself to think about something else—anything else. Absently, he rubbed her back, his thoughts racing. What the hell? Sure, he'd thought Raine was stunning when he'd first arrived at Shadows. Her inky hair and eloquent blue eyes turned heads every night. But now that he had her close, everything about her called not only to the Dom in him, but to the man as well. He needed to get his head screwed on straight, for Hammer's sake.

"It isn't your fault. You care for Hammer, and he's…well, he's got a few issues he needs to be sorting out, for sure. While he does, wouldn't you like to learn about true submission so you might be ready for him? Have you ever wished to stretch a bit, find out if you truly have the courage to submit?"

The way her breath caught before she blushed and jerked her gaze to the floor again suggested that his idea intrigued her.

Liam curled a finger under her chin, raising her face to his once more, and had to steel himself against another shocking jolt of lust. "You have, haven't you?"

"I want to be what Hammer needs, but I don't know for certain that I have the self-discipline to kneel and hold my tongue. I've never had the opportunity to try." She swallowed, honesty paining her expression. "But I still don't understand what's in it for you."

"You're a beauty, for sure. Touching you will be no hardship, lass." Right now, he hated how true that was. "From what I've seen, you can be a mouthy wench who would benefit from a red ass now and again." He forced himself to wink and grin.

After a split second of waiting for her reaction, her eyes flashed wide. Then she bestowed on him the sweetest sound he'd heard in months, her unbridled laughter.

"There's a girl." His smile became real. "Let me help you. I see your need. I enjoy molding and teaching." He cupped her cheek. "You should be cherished and nurtured, and I'd be honored to give that to you, Raine. Are you game?"

Indecision washed over her face. Liam found himself holding his breath, praying she'd say yes. Hammer needed her…and Liam staggered with his own need to touch her—at least once. It wasn't noble, and he wasn't proud of it. But she was so damn fuckable, and he was just a man. This lust would pass.

"You don't seem like the sort to do something halfway. You'll want to lay my soul bare, won't you? Make me show you all the broken parts?" She crossed her arms over her chest, nudging him back. "If I show you, are you going to run like Hammer, too?"

He uncrossed her arms and leaned closer. Now he could hear her softly indrawn breaths, see her fine trembling. Desire surged. Liam couldn't stop himself; he curled a hand around her shoulder, eliminating her personal space, and brushed his palm down to fasten on the curve of her waist. "I never run from a challenge I've set my mind on. Yes, I intend to split your soul wide open like a ripe peach, study you until I know well every piece of the intriguing puzzle you are, down to the last detail, lovely. Then, I mean to put you back together with my touch and make it worth your while."

Raine looked half terrified. "Wow, that's awfully honest."

"Best to set the expectation up front."

She let out a deep breath and fidgeted, trying to drop her gaze once more. He didn't allow it, lifting her chin again and bending until their eyes met. "Answer me, Raine. Yes or no?"

"I-I've wanted a good Dom. I thought it would be Hammer, but…" She closed her eyes and frowned.

Liam bit his tongue. She wanted to feel valued above all else— needed it. He tucked that knowledge in the back of his head and let her continue. "But?"

"I can't be less than honest with you. You know where my heart is. As much as I would love to explore everything you could teach me—really, I would—I don't know if I could give you the devotion you deserve. And I doubt Hammer would ever give his consent, even for you. It might be better for us all if I just left."

He trapped her against the counter in an instant, pressing his body to hers. Her lips parted in question. Her wide gaze jumped to his, then she focused on his mouth. An electric jolt rattled down his spine. Damn, she was potent.

Yanking her soft curves flush against the hard ridges of his body, he ached to dig his fingers into her hair, pull her lips under his, and eat away at her mouth until she moaned. Liam forced himself to stop. This wasn't about him, but Hammer. And Raine.

Dragging in a rough breath, he palmed her nape tenderly with one hand, fingers teasing the perfect pink shell of her ear with the other before trailing down to caress her throat. Finally, he settled his hand on her chest, just above her plump breast. Her breathing changed to soft pants. He could feel her heart beating madly under his palm. She wasn't immune to him. An intoxicating rush of power filled him.

Then he took her wrists in his free hand and brought her arms up slowly, bracing them against the cabinets above, her breath caught. A triumph he didn't welcome spiked inside him. Still, he bent to Raine, giving her ample time to push him away. She didn't. Her tongue swept nervously across her upper lip. His cock jerked. Then he couldn't stop himself from seizing her mouth with his own, capturing her gasp.

Soft. So fucking soft. And sweet. Bloody hell... Pleasure fired through his blood like a potent drug as he delved inside. She melted beneath him.

Curling his tongue around hers, he feasted on her addicting flavor, hungry to memorize it. One kiss melted into the next, and he devoured her, inhaling her into his lungs. She turned to liquid desire against him, wild and tumultuous. One leg slid surreptitiously around his, capturing his calf, pulling him in tighter against her small frame, splitting her thighs open. He should pass up that perfect invitation, but he didn't. Instead, he ground himself against her pussy, leaving her no doubt that he desired her. Despite Raine's little skirt, her flesh burned him. A low groan ripped from his throat. He didn't need air or space or tomorrow, just more of her. Right fucking now.

THEIR VIRGIN CONCUBINE
Masters of Ménage, book 3
Available Now
By Shayla Black and Lexi Blake

The country of Bezakistan – renowned for its wealth and the beauty of its deserts

Piper Glen is thrilled when Rafe and Kade al Mussad ask her to visit their country on a business trip. Madly attracted to both, the virginal secretary knows that neither of her intensely handsome bosses desires her. But every night she dreams of having them both in her bed, fulfilling her every need.

Rafe and Kade have finally found the perfect woman in Piper. Sweet and funny. Intelligent and strong. Before they can reveal their feelings, the brothers must fulfill an ancient tradition. Every sheikh must steal his bride and share her with his brothers. They have thirty days to convince Piper to love them all forever.

The country of Bezakistan – notorious for its danger…

Sheikh Talib al Mussad knows his villainous cousin seeks to take his throne. If Talib and his brothers fail to convince the beautiful Piper to love them, all will be lost. After meeting Piper, he knows he would risk everything to possess her heart.

Khalil al Bashir has long coveted his cousin's rule. Without a bride to seal their birthright, his every wish will come true. If Piper falls for them, he will lose everything but Piper can't love them if she's dead…

EXCERPT

Tal stared out. The limo must have pulled up while he was wishing he could choke the breath out of Khalil. He couldn't miss the woman Cooper spoke about. She wore a sundress, the delicate material flowing around her knees like a handkerchief blowing in a summer breeze. On her feet were a pair of yellow heels. Stilettos. He was a sucker for stilettos. He especially loved them when they were settled on either side of his neck as he fucked his way into a soft, hot pussy.

His breath caught. His entire body stiffened, especially his cock. She was lovely. So soft. Her hair was brown, but shot through with reds and blondes that caught the light and practically gave her a damn halo. Except nowhere, in any ancient text, did angels have cleavage like hers. The dress had been selected to show off her plump, ripe breasts, the V-neck and the turquoise color of the gauzy material flattering her skin. She had on a pair of sunglasses, but even without seeing her eyes, he could tell she was gawking. Her gorgeous, full lips were slightly parted in awe as she took in the sights. Her mouth looked small. He would likely have to force his cock in, but she would have that same look on her face when she came.

Tal had to catch himself. What was he doing? His bride was here, and he was reacting to some bimbo his brothers had brought along. A gathering rage rode through his system. This had to be Kadir's doing. Rafiq wouldn't think to bring his latest girlfriend along when they were supposed to be focused on securing a bride.

Sure enough his youngest brother got out of the limo and was immediately all over the brunette.

His heart sank. Poor Piper. Had she been forced to watch Kade's behavior the whole trip? Was this how his brother meant to show him he wouldn't accept Tal's choice of bride?

"I will kill him." Piper deserved better than Kade's scorn. She might not be the most beautiful woman in the world, but she was sweet and smart and he was actually looking forward to having her as a companion. Over the last few months, he'd grown closer to the woman than any he had in years. He appreciated her quick wit and her soft heart. The woman with Kade was beautiful, but she likely didn't have half of Piper Glen's smarts. She might make his dick hard, but Piper would be his wife. *Their* wife. He would never allow his youngest brother to dishonor her this way again.

"Oh, wow. Uhm, boss, you told us she was kind of homely. We have two different versions of that word, man." Dane shook his head as Rafiq joined Kadir.

Rafe, his ultimately reasonable brother, the one he counted on, walked right up to Kade's little bit of honey-on-the-side and pulled her into his arms. He kissed her, his lips molding to hers before he broke it off and smiled. Rafe pointed up as he talked to her.

Tal knew exactly what his brother was saying. He was pointing out the architecture on the palace. He gave every visitor the same speech about the marble and arches, and the center of the palace that dated from the fifteenth century. But now he gave the speech with an intimate smile on his face as his hands tangled with the brunette's.

Rafe wouldn't dishonor their promised bride. Rafiq believed in his country's traditions. He was circumspect.

So…that gorgeous, curvy thing was his Piper?

Dane huffed behind him. "Holy shit, Tal. If she's your little smarty-pants bride, she doesn't look like an egghead."

Tal strode forward, his heart racing. No way. He'd seen her pictures. She was plain. She would engage his brain but not his heart. Careful. He'd been so fucking careful.

"Rafe?" He called out to his infinitely more reasonable brother. "The trip went well?"

Introduce me to my plain but brilliant bride. Tell me she's shy and still in the limo.

Kade's arm tightened around the brunette's waist. "Talib! It's good to see you."

He stopped, halting a few feet before her. "And you, brother." His youngest brother was the wild one. He loved Kadir. He did, but he worried about him, too. Still, he couldn't help but notice the way his youngest brother's hand slipped into the brunette's and her fingers curled around his.

"Talib, it is my greatest pleasure to introduce you to…" Don't say Piper. Don't say Piper. "…Piper Glen. I believe you two have been speaking. Piper, *habibti*, this is our brother, his Serene and Royal Highness the Sheikh of Bezakistan, otherwise known as Talib al Mussad."

She freed her hand and pulled her sunglasses off. Her blue eyes went wide and that truly magnificent chest swelled. "Tal?"

Fuck. Fuck. Fucking fuck fuck fuck and a goddamn fucking duck. He'd only heard her voice a few times, but it was imprinted on his brain. That soft Texas twang with the hint of smarts and vulnerability. Piper. His Piper. His goddamn fucking virginal bride who would be his companion and who would rarely tempt his cock but never once move his soul.

Both were completely poleaxed because she was so beautiful.

"Hello, Piper. Yes, I am Sheikh Talib al Mussad. Or Tal, if you please." There was nothing else to do. He had to introduce himself. Funny. He'd thought this would be a prideful moment when he revealed himself to be so much more than she'd expected, and he found himself almost shy. He didn't show it, of course.

Her blue eyes took him in. "Talib. Of course. How stupid of me, but then I have been for months, it seems." She stopped, her shoulders slumping a little. "Or am I wrong? Are you my Tal?"

This was supposed to be a special moment, when she looked up to him. Instead, she looked betrayed. "Yes. I am Tal, Piper. How is your sister?"

He knew everything about her. He knew about her family and her love for Mindy. He'd already taken care of the girl's education, though Piper wouldn't realize that for a few days. He knew about his bride's upbringing. He knew what she liked and what she didn't.

Until now, he hadn't known how her eyes would pierce through him and see straight to his soul. He hadn't known how his cock would pound at the very sight of her.

Her whole face contorted as if in pain. "You're the third brother?"

Why did guilt roil in his gut? "Yes. It is good to meet you in person. I have enjoyed our talks over the internet. I am very eager to continue our discussions now that you are here."

Her eyes dropped away, studying the ground in front of her. She didn't pull away from his brothers, but he could feel her confusion.

"You're the sheikh?" Her voice was a bleak monotone. "And you let me think you were just another researcher."

He couldn't let her win this argument. If he allowed his guilt to show, she would have the upper hand. It wasn't how he intended to begin a marriage. "Bezakistan is my country. I didn't lie to you, Piper. I work very hard for my country. This project means the world to me."

"Of course. I'd like to go to my apartment, please. When would you like my presentation? I need a few hours to settle in and get everything in order." She was cool and competent, that flustery feminine energy from before fleeing, leaving a somber woman in its place.

"Don't worry about that right now," Kade said. "You need to rest, *habibti*."

"I will show you to your rooms. Don't be angry with us. Let us explain about security measures. Talib cannot simply tell everyone who he is. And he really does the work he said he does. He has a master's degree in economics." Rafe's hand tangled in hers.

Her eyes went up, taking in the grandeur of the palace. "This is where I'm staying? Well, naturally." Sarcasm dripped, and she looked furious. Closed. "I'd like to rest now. I want to get my presentation ready. And what we discussed on the plane? It won't work. I'm not that girl. So you all need to rethink this because if I'm here for any reason other than the job, then I should just buy a plane ticket now and head home as soon as my presentation is over."

Oh, she was here for a job. She was here for the most important job he could think of. She was here to be their wife, to save his throne. It didn't matter how much she moved his cock. He had a crown to think of. She was going to be theirs. Her beauty and innate sensuality that tempted him so were problems he would deal with later.

He caught sight of Khalil, stalking behind the palace walls, his stare taking in Piper.

This was precisely why he hadn't wanted a woman who would move him. The idea of Khalil even looking at her as a potential way to get under his skin had his blood pressure rising. It would be hard enough to protect her with a cool head, but if his emotions came into play? He had to shield her from being a target for rebels and neighboring radicals. Everything rested on her soft shoulders.

He needed her wedded and bedded and pregnant as quickly as possible. He had no intention of hurting her, but he had no intention of letting her go.

"Please, allow me to show you to your rooms." It was time, perhaps, to play on everything he knew about her. "I apologize for the subterfuge. I wanted a thought partner in this process. Can you honestly tell me you would have spoken as openly as you did with me had you known who I am?"

Her eyes flared a little and then slid away from his. "Probably not. I think I called you an idiot on a couple of occasions."

He brought his fingers to her chin, forcing her to look up at him. "My math was faulty, and yours was correct. And you called me an ape with my head up my backside because I was being stubborn when you knew you were right." He sighed a little, letting his face fall, noting all the while that she utterly softened with every layer of guilt he heaped on her. "I loved our talks, Piper. Ask anyone in the palace. I set aside that time to work with you, and it was sacred. I walked out on a conference with the British Prime Minister because I had a call scheduled with you."

Yes, she was flustered again and that was right where he wanted her. And Rafe was a bastard because there was no doubt he'd dressed her for this occasion. The brilliantly colored sundress was lovely and modest, but he couldn't miss the swells of her breasts and the way her skin caught the sunlight. Rafe had trussed her up like a gorgeous bird ripe for the plucking.

"I would have waited," she murmured.

"But I could not." He let his hand drop. He was actually surprised that when he looked back on the incident, he meant every word he said. He could remember sitting there listening to the Prime Minister talk about deeply important issues and he'd been watching the clock, waiting for the seconds to tick by until he could talk to her, her slow accent soothing him. He sighed. "It does not matter. I will admit I brought you here for selfish reasons. I thought to dazzle you with everything I have to offer. I have obviously failed."

That gorgeous skin flushed, and he knew he had her. She just stared at him, clearly uncertain what to say.

"I will leave you be, Miss Glen. Again, I apologize for the deception. I can only hide behind my desire to begin a relationship on equal ground. Please allow my brothers to show you to the rooms I have prepared for you. I will leave you be until such time as we conduct business. I wish you good rest and please enjoy my country."

Tears pooled in her eyes, but he couldn't let those sway him. It was time to make his exit and allow the wonders of the palace and her own soft heart to work in his favor. He bowed politely and turned to go, Dane stepping in beside him, Landon and Cooper in flanking positions.

The big former SEAL had a frown on his face. "That was a pretty piece of manipulation if I ever saw one. You're a ruthless son of a bitch, Tal."

He walked forward. Dane wouldn't be the last person he pissed off. By the time this was over, he might lose everyone.

But he would keep his crown. One way or another.

A DOM IS FOREVER
Masters and Mercenaries, book 3
Available Now
By Lexi Blake

A Man with a Past...

Liam O'Donnell fled his native Ireland years ago after one of his missions ended in tragedy and he was accused of killing several of his fellow agents. Shrouded in mystery, Liam can't remember that fateful night. He came to the United States in disgrace, seeking redemption for crimes he may or may not have committed. But the hunt for an international terrorist leads him to London and right back into the world he left behind.

A Woman Looking for a Future...

Avery Charles followed her boss to London, eager to help the philanthropist with his many charities. When she meets a mysterious man who promises to show her London's fetish scene, she can't help but indulge in her darkest fantasies. Liam becomes her Dom, her protector, her lover. She opens her heart and her home to him, only to discover he's a man on a mission and she's just a means to an end.

When Avery's boss leads them to the traitorous Mr. Black, Liam must put together the puzzle of his past or Avery might not have a future...

EXCERPT

"I want you." She wanted him so badly. She just didn't trust that he could possibly want her.

"No, you don't, but you will." He stepped back and tucked his shirt in. "We're going to do this my way. We tried yours and it didn't work, so I'm taking control. I should have done it in the first place. If I thought you had some, I would tell you to change into fet wear, but you don't happen to have a corset and some PVC hiding in that closet, do you?"

"I don't know what PVC is," she admitted, her heart aching a little. "I don't think this is a good idea, Lee. I don't think I can be what you need. I'm not experienced, and what experience I have wasn't very good. Don't get me wrong. I loved my husband, but the sex wasn't spectacular. I think I'm just one of those women who can't be sexy. I was trying to please you, but I couldn't."

Even in the dim light, she could see him staring, assessing. "And I think you're one of those women who can't stop thinking long enough to let her body take over. Look, Avery, the sex you've had happened with a kid. Was your husband older than you? More experienced?"

She shook her head. They had both been virgins.

"Then you have no idea what it can be like. I look at sex differently than most people. It's an exchange, and it should be good for both parties. I don't want you to spread your legs and let me have you because you want someone to hold you. If you want me to hold you, ask me. I want you to spread your legs because you can't wait another single second for my cock. I want that pussy ripe and ready and weeping for a big dick to split it wide and have its way. I want your nipples to peak because I walk into a room and you remember every dirty thing I can do to them. I want you to want me. I can make you crave me. I don't want some drive-by fucking that gets me off and I forget it five minutes later. I want to fuck all night long. I want to feel it all the next day because my cock got so used to being deep inside your body. If that's what you want, then get dressed in the sexiest thing you own and agree that I'm the boss when it comes to sex." He turned and walked out. "I'll give you five minutes to decide. I'll be waiting in your living room. If you really want me, you'll dress exactly how I've told you to dress and you'll present yourself to me for inspection. And Avery, no bra and no underwear. You won't need them."

The door closed behind him, and she had to remember how to breathe.

She wasn't sexy. She wasn't orgasmic.

But what if she could be? Lee hadn't been right about everything, but he had a few points. He'd told her he wanted to be in control and then she'd tried to make all the decisions. He had more experience, but she'd decided she knew best. She hadn't listened to him.

He wanted control. He wanted her to really want him. She didn't understand, but if she ever wanted to understand, she had to try.

She'd taught herself how to walk again. That had been an enormous mountain to climb. Why was she so scared of this? She'd faced worse, but she was cowering in her boots over not wearing underwear and a bra? She'd lost so much. Was she willing to lose this, too?

What was she really risking? She might look dumb. She could end up with her heart broken, but at least she would have proven it still worked.

She'd come across the ocean to change her life—to have a life. What was life without a few risks?

She got her phone out and sent a quick text to Adam letting him know she was home and who she was with so if she was serially murdered, at least they would have a starting place for where to find her body.

But she was going to do this because she felt safe with Lee. And because she wanted to finally understand what it really meant to want someone.

For more information, visit www.LexiBlake.net.

CPSIA information can be obtained at www.ICGtesting.com
Printed in the USA
LVOW06s1823091013

356189LV00001B/209/P